Lillian Beckwith was b[...]
in 1916. Her father's grocer[...]
for her autobiographical [...]
which describes a 1920s family from a child's viewpoint.

She went to live in the Hebrides before the Second World War and stayed for nearly twenty years. Her hilarious initiation into crofting life is captured in the heart-warming book *The Hills Is Lonely*. She acquired her own cottage, and living and working on her own croft gave rise to her series of magical Hebridean books such as *The Sea for Breakfast*. She now lives on the Isle of Man.

A Breath of Autumn

Lillian Beckwith

HOUSE OF
STRATUS

This edition published in 2002 by House of Stratus, an imprint of House of Stratus Ltd, Thirsk Industrial Park, York Road, Thirsk, North Yorkshire, YO7 3BX, UK.

www.houseofstratus.com

Typeset by House of Stratus, printed and bound by Short Run Press Limited.

A catalogue record for this book is available from the British Library and the Library of Congress.

ISBN 0-7551-1350-0

To the people of the Western Isles of Scotland
who have added so richly to my life

Vocabulary

Mor (More)	*big*
Beag (Bek)	*small*
Prapach (Prapak)	*a small pile of hay*
Poc (Pok)	*a bag or sack*
Ceilidh (Kayley)	*a meeting of folk for gossip and song*
Strupach (Stroopak)	*a cup of tea and a bite to eat*
Mo ghaoil (Moh gool)	*my dear*
Bodach (Botak)	*old man*
Cailleach (Kalyak)	*old woman (the wife)*
Cas chrom (Kas krowm)	*the Hebridean foot plough*
Skart	*the shag or green cormorant*
Oidhche mhath (Oykee va)	*good night*
Creagach (Kraykak)	*sea wrasse (a fish)*
Slainte mhath (Slanjy va)	*good health*
Potach (Potak)	*a cake made from oatmeal, water and\or whisky*

Souming	*the number of animals a crofter is permitted to keep on his croft*
Beannachd leat (Bianak let)	*blessings go with you*
Lobhta (Lofta)	*loft*
Salachar	*filthy (of a person)*
Crotal	*a lichen used for dying cloth*
Trodhd (Tro-art)	*come here*
Tapadh leat (Tapa let)	*thank you*

chapter one

Kirsty MacDonald settled herself on the rock that protruded like a sill from the heathery bank of moorland beside the sheep track. Raising her binoculars, she scanned the rugged outline of the island that lay a mile or so across the Sound, focusing on the wide-mouthed bay whose shingle shore gave the appearance of being the threshold of the irregular line of croft houses that comprised the village of Clachan. After a few moments, she swung her gaze to the schoolhouse which, even at that distance, was easily identifiable. Set against the starkly rising cliffs at one end of the bay, it had a high-pitched roof, narrow institutionalised windows, and a tiny uncluttered playground enclosed by a sturdy stone wall which defended it from the sea. The school had a distinct air of aloofness, as if it had been designed to create the impression that it was drawing away the hem of its garments from the squat thatched croft houses with their adjoining unkempt byres and barns, their decrepit hen-houses and incongruously neat peat stacks and haystacks. For some minutes her gaze rested on the schoolhouse as if she might be seeking to detect some sign of activity, yet she well knew that her binoculars were not sufficiently powerful to discern movement at such a

1

distance. Her eyes began to water and, with a sigh, she lowered the glasses, blinked rapidly, and continued to stare across the Sound, her mind preoccupied by how her son, the Wee Ruari as he'd always been known, was reacting to his first day of formal education.

She herself had taken him across the Sound to Clachan earlier that morning in *Katy*, the dinghy with the outboard motor and, sensitive to his husky entreaty that there should be no motherly embrace or fond farewell, they'd parted from each other with no more than a muttered whisper of 'Beannachd leat', a nod, and a tightly controlled smile. Again at his insistence, she'd stayed beside the *Katy*, pretending to be adjusting the floorboards while she covertly watched him make his way over the shingle and up to the entrance of the school playground, where already several scholars of varying ages and sizes were clustered, eyeing the newcomer's approach with evident interest. It was the first time that mother and son had been parted for more than an hour or so and now, from today, they would be unlikely to see each other until the following Friday evening, and only then if the sea were calm enough for someone to take the *Katy* across to get him.

The realisation that her son was approaching the age when he would need to go to school, and that when that time came he would have to live much of the time away from her, had been a lurking disquiet in her mind for many months. It was not that she hadn't been keen for him to be educated in a school with other children, yet when Jamie, her stepson, had said bluntly one day, 'Isn't it time Wee Ruari was starting school and being more with children of his own age?' the question had stunned her momentarily: it had sounded so brusque.

2

'Time enough,' she'd said, trying to make her voice sound bland, so Jamie would not suspect her uneasiness, but Wee Ruari, having heard Jamie put the question, had since given her little respite from his demands to know how long he must wait before he could go to school. He was ready for school, he'd declared positively, and she had to acknowledge to herself he was certainly that. He might not have reached the required age to start, but his keenness to learn had been evident from his earliest years. As soon as his small fingers had become nimble enough to manage a pencil she had taught him firstly how to copy a few simple letters and then how to link them so that they spelled simple three-letter words. On winter afternoons, in the quiet time after she'd fed the hens and before 'the boys', as she referred to Jamie and his crewman Euan Ally, had returned from their fishing, it had become the custom for her to read to him from one of the children's story-books which she'd requested from the mainland library and which Jamie regularly collected from the post office every couple of months. The books were far too advanced for Wee Ruari to read himself, but once the lamp was lit he loved to sit at the table, as close as possible to her, seemingly fascinated by the lines of black printing, which her voice could turn magically into stories of other children, other animals, other lands far beyond the hills, beyond the sea and sometimes, as she would try to explain, beyond the sunset.

His learning had been further advanced by a gift of more suitable books from a young couple who, while holidaying in Clachan the previous summer, had managed to persuade a boat-owner to ferry them over to Westisle. They had become so enchanted with its secluded glens and hidden corries, its undisturbed moorland, the variety of plant life and wildlife, that they had asked if they might bring over their tent and spend the remainder of their holiday encamped in the shelter of one of the derelict cottages. It was a cottage which at one time had been the home of crofters. She'd agreed, a little reluctantly at first because they were English, and the English were regarded by the islanders as being proud and unfriendly. She'd feared they might prove to be a nuisance but, to her surprise, she'd found she much enjoyed their presence and when, at the end of their stay, they had asked if they could make a similar arrangement for the following year and stay for the whole of their holiday she'd acquiesced unhesitatingly. It had turned out that the young woman was a primary-school teacher and her husband a university lecturer. When they'd arrived the following spring they'd brought with them a parcel of beautifully illustrated books of rhymes and stories for Wee Ruari, who was so taken with the gift he seemed to think that in return he should escort them to wherever they wished to go on the island and show them some of his favourite places. Kirsty, anxious that he should not be a nuisance to them, had tried to dissuade him from seeking their company too frequently, explaining to him that they wanted to be left alone to quietly explore the island and seek specimens of plants and pebbles to take back to England with them. Somewhat reluctantly, he'd agreed.

It was inevitable that, after the couple had been encamped for a few days, a fierce gale accompanied by lashing rain had wreaked havoc on their camp and Kirsty, who, from the moment of their arrival had been prepared for such an eventuality, had offered them instead the shelter of her unused loft room. It was likely they would be cosy enough in their sleeping bags in her house. Wee Ruari had been overjoyed that they should all be together in the same house and the young woman, whose name was Polly, had been so much taken with his eagerness to learn that, when she had not been helping her husband classify specimens, she'd been happy to read to the boy, frequently encouraging him by moving her finger below the words as she read. She'd also taught him some English nursery rhymes and had been delighted when he repeated them to her almost without hesitation. Though he'd given every impression of enjoying them, he'd confided to Kirsty that English children must be 'pretty daft' to believe that such silly rhymes 'schooled' them as he put it, but both she and Jamie had subsequently suffered many days, weeks, and months of hearing the singsong repetition of 'Bo-Peep', 'Simple Simon', and 'Little Boy Blue' which had never impinged upon their own early education.

Yes, Wee Ruari was certainly ready for school, Kirsty assured herself and, since he was 'no bauthalain' as her late husband used to declare, she was certain he would prove to be a scholar of whom she and the dominie would be proud. Waving away a hovering bumble bee, she directed her glasses on the 'Widow Fraser's' reed-thatched cottage which crouched snugly at the opposite end of the bay from the school. The 'Widow Fraser' was, in Kirsty's opinion, a worthy kind of woman: clean, hard-working and a good enough cook. When Kirsty had first spoken to her about having Wee Ruari to stay with her during the week when he would be attending school she had greeted the suggestion warmly. Having been a widow for nearly fifteen years and with her only child, a daughter, married and living in New Zealand, she'd welcomed the prospect of anyone, even a youngster, to keep her company and had appeared to be well satisfied with the small recompense Kirsty had been able to offer in return for his lodging.

So Kirsty had no reason for any misgivings about being parted from her son. She had spoken to the dominie some weeks previously and had been assured that 'the boy would be suitably supervised'. He would already be familiar with those of the scholars who had managed to coax their way onto a summer beachcombing expedition on Westisle, or perhaps had been counted useful enough to accompany a rabbit-shooting trip during the winter. The rest of the scholars would no doubt have been informed by the dominie that the new boy from Westisle would be joining the class when the new term started. There would, Kirsty imagined, be the initial wary reserve which was natural to all island children but it would speedily disperse and he would make good friends. He was that kind of boy just. She had no apprehensions as to his safety. She had taught him to swim, and the terrain of Westisle had conditioned him to cope with any hazards he might encounter in the not-too-dissimilar surroundings of Clachan, and yet she was still tense. 'I'm only deluding myself thinking it's just the separation from my son that is affecting me like this,' she reasoned. 'I'm just loath to allow myself to admit that the wrench of separation from him is aggravating the still raw wound that has ravaged me since the loss of my husband.' It was not, she had to admit, the loss of the kind and gentle man who had been Wee Ruari's father and who had tragically drowned before he had even known of the child that was in her womb, but the loss of his dour brother, the man who had subsequently offered her marriage without any semblance of affection but simply to ensure that she and her child could be sure of a permanent home. The man who, not until the final hours of his last illness, had confessed his secret and abiding love for her, and had, by doing so, unmasked her own love for him; a love which hitherto she had either smothered or had shrunk from recognising. But that love had been a secret between the two of them and because she thought of it as being in some way illicit she had, since his death, striven to maintain a stoical composure. Her shoulders sagged at the memory of that last farewell; her stoicism seemed to be deserting her and when she again tried to raise the glasses and focus them her hands were too unsteady. Her breath started to catch in her dry throat; her breast began to heave uncontrollably. 'Dear Lord, I'm too old to cry,' she chided herself; but grief was threatening to overwhelm her and, before she could get a grip on herself, even before she could grab a hasty handful of the overall beneath her jacket to staunch them, the tears were gushing from her eyes and running down her cheeks, blinding her. Shuddering, she turned away from the loch and from the hills, as if fearing that they were secretly spying on her.

Rolling onto her stomach, she pressed her yielding body into the conformity of the heather; sobs shook her as she tried to deceive herself into imagining it to be the close embrace she had yearned so much to receive.

Thus, completely alone, the twice-widowed Kirsty Mac-Donald at last abandoned herself to the grief she had for too long suppressed.

chapter two

How long her spell of anguish lasted she had little idea but it was a more persistent bumble bee that, finding her tear-damp face worth investigating, recalled her to the present and, though she had no fear that the bee might sting her, it served as a reminder of the urgency of the day's work. Weakened by grief, she nevertheless rose determinedly to her feet and started back along the track to the house, assuring herself that a good strong cup of tea would soon revive her crushed spirits. Before she had covered more than a few yards, however, her attention became riveted on the concentration of gannets over the loch. The birds had not been there earlier, and their presence brought her to an abrupt halt.

The annual arrival of the big white birds over the blue water was for her always an intriguing sight. Welcome too since it indicated the arrival of the annual shoals of herring, 'the silver darlings' as the crofters called them, with the promise of good fishing and subsequently a good stock of herring for salting down into barrels for winter food for the family; for those beasts which would eat them and, hopefully, some surplus for the baiting of the coming season's lobster creels. She permitted herself to linger for a while, captivated by the birds' swift, sleek diving, the noise curiously reminiscent of flat wooden boards being dropped on the water. She recollected her early childhood on her granny's croft, rejoicing in the remembered excitement which had infected the village when the gannets were first observed to be reconnoitring the nearby loch. 'It looks like the silver darlings are here!' the tidings had quickly circulated throughout the village proving to be the stimulus for every man who owned a dinghy to drop whatever he was doing and, be he nearly crippled with arthritis, or be his dinghy perilously held together by little more than tar and string and the mercy of God, to seek out his net. As the evening approached he would load it into the dinghy which, often with the willing assistance of a couple of equal decrepits, would then be dragged down to the tide and rowed out to the middle of the loch, there to wait tensely listening for the splashing rustle of a tight-packed shoal.

Each crofter cherished his own 'piece of net'. This was usually stored along with ancient clothes and archaic tackle 'up in the lobhta' which, since it frequently served as sleeping quarters for less particular, or less continent relatives of the family, ensured the net was well protected, from the ravages of moths by copious doses of urine. Every autumn when the arrival of the herring was being predicted the 'piece of net' would be brought out and examined and then attached with what Kirsty imagined to be prehistoric lengths of rope to a varied selection of buoys and floats gleaned from the flotsam and jetsam off the shore, and stored among an accumulation of lobster creels awaiting repair, discarded whelk sacks and matted, unusable sheep fleece in a corner of a byre or barn.

The herring could be expected to stay in the loch for perhaps three or four days and, day after day, night after night, the men devoted themselves to netting the sea's bounty; often snatching no more than an hour's sleep between catches and taking no other sustenance than an oatmeal potach and a wee dram of whisky. Yet they vehemently denied any feeling of tiredness or hunger. 'Ach a man needs neither food nor sleep when the "silver darlings" are in the loch asking to be caught, supposing they would be here for a week or more,' they maintained. Finally, they shed their damp clothes that still glistened with herring scales like miniature chain-mail. They would then take to their beds while their wives rinsed their clothes in the nearest burn and spread them out to dry.

Though they were never allowed near a dinghy, the excitement of the herring shoaling had infected the children of the village; an excitement from which Kirsty had felt a little excluded. Though most could at least claim kinship with the owner of some sort of boat, alas the only boat Kirsty's granny could lay claim to was the sadly disintegrating remains of one that, for as long as Kirsty could remember, had remained upside down outside the cow-byre, providing indifferent shelter for the odd broody hen and her chicks. In those days her granny had been forced to rely on the goodwill of neighbours to provide the family's winter store of herring. But Kirsty could not remember their ever going short.

She continued to retrace her path to the house, her attention divided between the gannets and the drifts of tiny butterflies, blue as a robin's egg, which, as she walked, rose like blue chaff from the heather. This is a beautiful island and I am fortunate to be here, she reminded herself, trying to mute the sharp ache that remained so obstinately in her breast. Assessing the portents of the sky she assured herself that its earlier serenity, now lightly chalked with threads of static white clouds much as if scratched by the flying gannets, seemed to indicate that calm and sunshine would last at least until the night. She set herself to working out her schedule for the day. She had milked the cows early that morning before taking Wee Ruari across the Sound to school, but she knew there was an urgent need to get the winter stack built and thatched. There were also brambles, heavy with ripeness and begging to be picked and made into jams and puddings and pies, and there were potatoes waiting to be dug and clamped. She debated which of the three tasks she should embark upon, balancing the urgency of each against which would be the most satisfying to accomplish. Deciding that the completion of the haystack was the most imperative, as soon as she reached the house she made herself a cup of tea and stuffed a piece of girdle scone into her jacket pocket. Putting damp peats on the fire, she armed herself with a sickle and a length of rope from the barn and set off for the bog land at the far side of the island where there were always plenty of reeds for the cutting. It would be good to get the last of the hay stacked, she told herself as she walked. After a savage winter and a dilatory spring the grass had responded to a gentle summer by producing an abundant growth. The barn was already packed with sweet-smelling hay but there was still more grass already scythed and made into temporary prapachs awaiting incorporation into the winter stack. The week before he had started school, she and Wee Ruari had carried many of these small

11

prapachs and heaped them beside the barn where the stack was to be built. Jamie and Euan Ally had stated their intention only the previous evening of coming in early from their fishing if the weather held so as to start work on the winter stack well before nightfall. She reasoned that if she could cut and carry enough reeds it might even be possible to get the stack not only built but finally thatched and hopefully netted and securely roped before it grew too dark. She spurred herself to quicken her pace. The two Ruaris had never allowed her to help with the stack building. It was not women's work they maintained, shrugging off her suggestion as if she might be doubting their ability to accomplish the task without her help. She had been limited to providing strupaks whenever they were called for. Nevertheless it had been evident, in spite of their obvious tiredness, what a deeply satisfying achievement it had been for them when at last the stack was finished and they could step back and critically survey the sturdy bulk of it, assessing its firmness to withstand the on-slaught of the winter gales.

From her earliest days when she was a wee girl on her granny's croft she had loved to be around at stack-building time, revelling in the sweet all-encompassing smell of the mixture of seedy grasses and perceiving, young as she was, the compelling urgency to get the stack finished before the rain threatened or before the wind rose – an urgency which seemed to her always to have generated a spirit of elation rather than irritation among the stack builders; every remark eliciting a chuckled response; every slight mishap an airy dismissal. Since there had been no barn or shed on her granny's croft suitable for storing hay safe from rain and vermin, it all had to be built into a stack. When the chosen day came the hard labour of building had to begin as soon as the dew was off the grass. The work had continued unceasingly, save for a 'fly cup', until the stack was finished or dark had called a halt to the work. There'd been no time on stack-building day to think of 'stopping for potatoes', as the main meal of the day was known, and Kirsty still carried the mental image of her granny, once the task was completed, sagging with exhaustion and yet at the same time almost stately with exultation as she returned to the house to take at last the much longed for strupak.

She was determined to be of more use to 'the boys' since they would be tackling the job of stack building after a full day's fishing and, well conditioned to hard work as they might be, she was quite certain they would welcome any assistance she could give them. Once she had reached the bog lands she slashed hastily at a good clump of reeds, gathered them up, roped them into a fair-sized bundle and swung it onto her back. After only a short distance on the homeward path she realised the bundle was proving rather heavier than she had been prepared for and she felt in need of a rest. 'I'm getting soft,' she berated herself. 'Either that or I've got to face up to the fact that I'm not as strong as I used to be.' Dropping her load beside the path she turned towards the old crofter settlement, knowing of a good spring where she could cool her face and soothe her hot, dry throat. Once refreshed she chose an area of dry sward and sat down. Resting her back against a boulder she ate her piece of scone whilst scanning the bay. Ever since she had lived on the island, the old settlement had fascinated her.

Today the bay was quietly rippled and at the mouth of the burn a stately heron was poised, still as a sculpture, waiting patiently for the chance of a meal. Further out to sea, rafts of kittiwakes flew speculatively above and intermittently flopped into the water in pursuit of their elusive prey. There were several gannets too, she noticed, but their diving was only sporadic and she guessed that the bulk of the herring shoal must still be located at the other side of the island.

Her eye lit on the ancient, weed-encrusted marker buoy about a mile offshore which, during the hours of daylight, was almost always surmounted by a seabird of one species or another, more often than not a black-backed gull. The buoy, she had learned, had been there for countless years before the two Ruaris had been born and before anyone now alive could remember, yet it was still anchored and still undulating to the surge of the sea. She'd wondered what hazard the buoy marked. Was it some minor wreck? Why had it never been removed as, with neither bell nor light to indicate its presence, it was surely more of a hazard than a warning to shipping? The two Ruaris had not been concerned by its presence. It seemed unlikely that she would ever know though since she was now the owner of the island she supposed she could enquire from some official source. She shrugged off the thought, not being particularly interested. Lazily she contemplated the perched sea bird. It was, as she had expected, a black-backed gull. Her mind mulled lightly over the reason for it being there. Did it perhaps enjoy perching on the constantly swinging buoy as a respite from the equally constant cradling of the sea? Or did it simply enjoy contemplating its surroundings as she enjoyed contemplating it? She smiled as she switched her thoughts once again to the beauty of the island and the unforeseeable circumstances that had led to her being its owner.

She recalled her first husband, Ruari Beag, the younger of the two Ruaris, telling her how the story had begun when they had first met and conversed in the kitchen of Islay, the boarding house where she had worked for so many years until he had rescued her with his surprising offer of marriage. The man whom Ruari had named as 'the new laird' had at one time owned the whole estate of which the small island of Westisle was an insignificant part. The laird's son, rather a reckless young man had, it seemed, taken a great fancy to the island and had asked his father if he could take over that part of it which the crofters did not claim and farm it himself. Willingly the old man had not only granted his son's wish but had built for him a good stone house in the hope that the boy might marry and settle down. But, no sooner had the house been finished, war had broken out and the young man had gone off to be an officer. Alas, he had never returned and the grief-stricken father had shortly afterwards decided to dispose of the whole estate and return to England. But the island of Westisle, which his son had so loved, he offered to his shepherd, in recognition of his loyal service to his country and to his employer. The shepherd, who was by that time courting a young maid employed in the laird's kitchen, had taken a while to think about it. Owing to the harshness of the previous landlord, the old crofters had left the island, and he doubted if a young woman would be prepared to set up home in such isolation. When he'd put it to her however, she'd agreed without hesitation so they had ferried over a few cattle and sheep to the island and had settled in the newly completed house. It was there that the two Ruaris had been born.

She wondered how she herself would feel if she were forced to leave Westisle. It would be a dreadful wrench she knew, since it had become a much cherished home. She mentally catalogued its advantages. Good water; plenty of stone for building; a fair acreage of pasture; a good area of rough grazing for sheep and cows and also, here at the settlement there was a good shore from which it would be easy enough for just one person to launch a small dinghy to catch enough fish for a meal when desired. She acknowledged there weren't many good peat bogs but the peat island itself was not far away. She'd once asked Ruari Beag, her first husband, why he thought the old laird had not chosen to build the house for his son near the settlement instead of the far side of the island which she thought offered relatively few advantages. Her husband had dismissed the question in a tone of reproof. 'Ach, what laird would have wanted his son living so close to his tenants now, surely.'

'No, of course not,' she'd replied. It had taken only a fleeting moment for her to recollect the wide gap between rich lairds and their subjects no matter how well liked and respected the laird might be. I wouldn't have cared, she'd thought. I'd far sooner have lived near the settlement than where he built the house for his son. But she knew better than to voice her thoughts.

When she'd decided to stop for a rest she had not suspected that she was tired enough to let herself doze off, even for a minute or so, but when she again looked at the shore she was shocked to see that the tide line was a good

16

six feet lower than when she had been eating her scone. The heron had gone, the kittiwakes had transferred their attentions elsewhere. Hastily she rose to her feet and, once again hoisting the bundle of reeds onto her back, resumed her path to the house.

chapter three

'Ach, you have plenty of reeds already.' 'The boys' were home even earlier than she had expected and it was Jamie's voice greeting her. 'We was after thinking we'd need to go over to the bog-land and gather a bundle so we could maybe cap the stack before the last of the light. We've found enough old straw to make a base so we'll get started right away just.'

She prepared a strupak for them which they quickly bolted before rushing outside. It was good to see that they were as eager as herself to start work on building the winter stack, so she threw damp peats on the fire, tied a duster over her hair, a sack apron on top of her overall and, grabbing a hay-fork, hurried to join them. They were already treading down a layer of straw and rushes for the base.

'I was seeing plenty of gannets busying themselves over the loch earlier in the day,' she announced as she approached. Stabbing a forkful of hay she threw it to Jamie who was standing in the middle of the well firmed base.

'Is it gannets,' quipped Jamie. 'Why, there's that many gannets round the place we reckon there's that much herring in the loch they'll be swimming ashore and not waiting for anyone to net them.'

'I doubted but that you'd not be wanting to leave your own fishing and come back to build the stack,' she teased them lightly, knowing full well that their own fishing brought them ready money while, important as the annual herring shoals in the loch were to the crofters, the size of the shoals was relatively insignificant, seldom providing more than winter food and bait.

'Indeed, we had a mind not to, did we not Euan Ally?' returned Jamie, his eyebrows raised ironically.

'That was the way of it just,' agreed Euan Ally, keeping up the note of flippancy. 'But we thought we'd get no more of your good tea-bread if we didn't get this built before the rain came, so we decided we'd best try and please you, seeing you're mighty keen to see the cattle well fed. Anyway, there's plenty more fish in the sea.'

'We'll get the stack finished before dark and then we'll get back to sea,' Jamie said. 'The best fishing comes with the darkening, so we'll maybe stay at sea for the night.'

'You'll be gey tired,' she cautioned. 'You were away before first light this morning, were you not?'

'Ach, a boat's wasted on a man that's too tired to go fishing when there's plenty of fish for the taking,' scoffed Jamie derisively.

The stack rose slowly but steadily higher as Kirsty and Euan Ally continued to gather and throw up forkful after forkful of hay from the surrounding stooks to Jamie who, balanced on top of the stack, caught each load expertly in his wide-stretched arms. He spread the hay skilfully and then trod it so that the centre of the stack was well firmed and, aided by Euan Ally's intermittent combing with a hay rake, its sides sloped without detectable bulges. They worked hastily but nevertheless with a pride in their work, which was in no way concealed by the almost constant chaffing from Jamie on their tardiness, which in turn was nimbly countered by Euan Ally's insouciant comments on Jamie's lack of skill at shaping. A gentle smile hovered around Kirsty's mouth as she listened to their banter. She imagined it was as much a part of their life together at sea as it was on land. It was comforting to know that they remained such good companions, she reflected.

The stack was already more than half built before she caught a comment from Jamie that she was not throwing the hay high enough for him to catch. With dismay she came to realise that her shoulders and arms were indeed beginning to protest at the continuing toil. She tried to ease them by lifting and lowering them, pausing for a moment or two to rest on her hay-fork until Jamie, perceiving her, commanded from the stack, 'Ach, you get back to the house now! We'll maybe get on as well without you. It'll not be so long now before we're finished and we'll be needing a strupak then.'

'I'll stay a wee whiley,' she demurred.

Euan Ally snatched the fork from her and threw it towards the barn. 'Get you gone!' he ordered peremptorily.

'I should think you'll be gey tired yourselves,' she argued weakly as she moved a step or two away. 'You had a good day's fishing before you came to start here, did you not?' Euan Ally only grunted. 'Will you not let me bring a wee strupak out here to you,' she coaxed.

'No, no,' refused Jamie adamantly. 'We'll no be wantin' to waste what's left of the light and it's likely we'll be back at the house in the time it takes you to get it.'

She'd hardly noticed until he spoke that the light had started to dim. Not that it would get truly dark, since a promise of moonlight was revealing itself behind the mainland hills, but there was certainly a perceptible darkening of the twilight.

Shaking stray wisps of hay from her skirt she turned to go back to the house; half-way there she paused and, assessing their handiwork, called back to them approvingly, 'It's a good enough shape then.' It had never been in her nature to be lavish with praise, nor in their natures to accept it, and if they heard her comment neither of them made any acknowledgement.

Back in the kitchen she first banked up the still-smouldering fire with a few twigs and dry peats and then applied the bellows until there was a good show of flames. After lighting the lamp, she swung one of the big black kettles and the full soup pan over the fire and put plates of scones, oatcakes, butter and crowdie on the table. There was enough for half a dozen appetites she reckoned before, thankfully kicking off her heavy boots, she flopped into a chair.

When she opened her eyes again the kitchen was brightened by the dawn. She was vexed that she hadn't heard a sound of 'the boys' coming in for their food but that they had been was evident from the cleared table, the almost empty soup pan pushed back on the hob, the empty teapot and the crockery washed and put back on the dresser.

'Amn't I the fool,' she chided herself. 'Sleeping while they got their own strupak and after they'd got two days' work done in one.' Rising from her chair and without bothering to put on her boots she padded across to the door and stood in her stockinged feet on the stone threshold looking at the stack. It looked sturdy enough she thought, not only finished and securely capped with the reeds she had gathered but already buttressed with a few spars of driftwood. It would need more support against the strengthening gales of winter but there was time enough for that yet, she knew. Meanwhile she experienced a warm surge of excitement in the knowledge that there was plenty of hay secured to see the beasts through until they could once again fill their bellies with the good spring grass. They're a good pair of lads she acknowledged, looking towards the stack, and they've made a right good job of you.

Back in the kitchen she put on the kettle ready to make her own bowl of brose. I must see I get them a meal that will more than please them when they get back from the sea, she promised herself. Maybe I could bake them a bramble pie to finish off with. The thought had hardly crossed her mind before she was taking two of the largest pails, one for milk and one for the berries she hoped to collect, and setting off in the direction she expected the cattle would be and where she knew were the most fruitful bramble bushes.

The weather looked promising enough she judged, surveying the dove-grey clouds that were being shepherded gently over the mainland hills by a light breeze. Choosing to amble rather than spur herself into her more customary brisk pace, she allowed herself the occasional pause to inhale deeply the early dawn scents and the earthy autumnal smells of the moorland; to scan appreciatively the deepening tawniness of the heather; to catch an occasional glimpse of winter gentians cushioned discreetly in the grassy bank. Though heedless of the strident 'Go back! Go back!' warnings of startled grouse as they erupted from the heather it struck her that the population of these birds on this side of the island seemed to have increased considerably since the two Ruaris had passed on and she puzzled over the reason for it. She had no recollection of either of the brothers ever having spoken of shooting grouse nor indeed had they ever brought one home for her to cook. She hadn't thought this unusual since she herself had never in her life tasted grouse flesh so it had been easy for her to assume that they, like herself and her granny and her crofter acquaintances, had absorbed from childhood the tenet that grouse were 'gentry folks' food' and therefore must be shot only by 'gentry folks' bullets'. She wondered if the brothers' indoctrination had been so rigorous it had resulted in a genuine distaste for the flesh of the birds since, despite their being the indisputable lairds of the island, they had not, to her knowledge, ever touched a grouse. Then why, she pondered, had the numbers increased in the last year or two. She'd heard it said that the number of birds must be limited because too abundant a population would result in disease and possible starvation. This was certainly not to be desired so how, without shooting, had the brothers managed to keep the population down to a reasonable level? And since she was now undoubtedly the laird and responsible for the management of Westisle, how should she tackle the problem? She decided she must first consult 'the boys', though she thought it improbable they would have any advice to give her save to consult the factor who dealt with all the details of her inheritance. For a moment or two she toyed with the idea of asking Jamie to shoot one of the birds so that they could at least taste it before having to make any decision. They might even like it, but she dismissed the idea almost instantly.

Although the brambles were proffering themselves for the picking it was fairly late in the afternoon when, accompanied by the sound of corncrakes among the reeds, she started for home with her half pail of milk and a very full pail of berries. As she neared the house the hens, anxious for their evening feed, rushed eagerly to meet her, their feet thudding on the trodden earth as if they were shod.

A couple of hooded crows keeping watch above the hen-house cawed despairingly and flapped unhurriedly out of sight. There was no evidence of 'the boys' having returned, so as soon as she had disposed of her two pails and had fed the hens she took a fork from the end of the house and made for the still undug potato plot. Once there she lifted a pail of potatoes and pulled a large turnip. Back indoors she immediately banked up the fire with sticks and dry peats to ensure the oven would soon get hot enough to cook the meal she planned to have ready for them when they did return.

Though she always liked to ensure that they took plenty of scones, oatcakes and eggs to sustain them while they were away in the boat, there remained, at the back of her mind, a niggle of worry that they might have stowed the food a little thoughtlessly on board; perhaps the entrance to the tiny galley had not been sufficiently secured against an unexpectedly truculent sea; perhaps water had seeped unnoticed into one of the tiny lockers above an unused bunk, turning the good food into a messy pulp by the time they came to eat it. Neither of them had ever mentioned any such mishap having occurred but even if it had, she doubted if they would have admitted to it. It was hearing tales from other fishermen in other boats that had led to her concern and to her firm resolve that when they came ashore they would always find a meal they would think worth coming for.

The peats were glowing brightly as she put the big stock pan on the hob and set about skinning the skart which Jamie had shot a couple of days previously. Along with turnip and potatoes and a mealy pudding it would make a tasty casserole. When the oven was nicely hot she made the bramble-berry pie which, when well sugared and served with a jug of thick cream she had skimmed from the setting bowls the day before, would make an appetising last course. She doubted if there would be a single berry of it left by the time they went to bed.

While everything was cooking she got out the box iron and started on the basket of ironing which had been waiting for the best part of a week. But the meal was cooked and the ironing basket was empty and there was still no sign of 'the boys'. She was disappointed. Surely they'll be staying out the night now, she told herself, recalling the remark Jamie had tossed off when they were building the winter stack. She had not taken him very seriously at the time but it was plainly too late to expect them now. As she stowed the food away in the scullery she found herself having to stifle her own repetitive yawns and had to face the fact that she was flagging with weariness. After laying damp peats on the fire she lit a candle and was carrying it through to her bedroom when through the window she caught a glimpse of the 'Merry Dancers' pulsating in the night sky. Flinging open the outer door, she stood enchanted by the spectacular display. It was by no means a rare sight; she had seen it many times, but tonight it was too arresting to think of forsaking it for sleep. Forgetting her tiredness, she stood watching until the brilliant colours had been chased from the sky by the oncoming dawn. Only then did she seek her bed.

chapter four

She easily filled a second pail of brambles after milking the cattle the next morning. Since she planned to make jam with them before 'the boys' came home she wasted no time in getting back to the house. They were back earlier than she was expecting them.

'You're throwing good smells out of the door,' accused Euan Ally as he and Jamie kicked off their sea boots outside the kitchen.

'She's making jam, is she not?' explained Jamie.

'That indeed is what I am doing,' she agreed. 'And no doubt the time it has taken me to make it will be twice as long as it will take you two and Wee Ruari to eat the lot of it between you,' she retorted.

'There's nothing I like more than a few spoonfuls of warm jam straight from the jar,' Jamie enthused. 'How about you Euan Ally?' But Euan Ally had gone through to the scullery. Jamie threw down a mailbag onto the bench before going to the dresser drawer to root out a spoon but Kirsty raised a restraining hand.

'No, you will not then,' she told him sternly. 'It is a wee whiley only since I finished filling the jars and if you go now digging with your spoon you will not only find the

27

jam will scald your tongue but it will not keep so well in the jar.'

Jamie's eyebrows shot up exaggeratedly. 'Who's wanting it to keep,' he teased her. She frowned. 'Ach,' he pretended to grumble, replacing the spoon and closing the drawer. Picking up the mailbag he swung it towards her. 'We collected the mail today seein' we'll not be going to sea tomorrow,' he said. 'Me and Euan Ally have taken out ours, so it's all for you.' He grabbed a towel and went through to join Euan Ally in the scullery.

She glanced after him, a little surprised. The bag seemed unusually full. She expected it to contain one or two mail-order catalogues, probably promoting new veterinary products for cattle and sheep but as she tipped the contents onto the table she saw that in addition to the catalogues there was a parcel addressed to Wee Ruari and another parcel of books for herself. There was also an envelope addressed to her. She leafed quickly through the books which she thought would make promising reading but she only scanned the envelope briefly before putting it, still unopened, on the dresser. She'd received very few letters in her lifetime, whether in the city or on Westisle and had developed a curious reluctance to read them. She had guessed who the letter was from, and decided it could wait until 'the boys' had taken their meal.

Jamie returned from the scullery. 'So you have a letter,' he remarked, glancing towards the dresser.

'Indeed I have so,' she replied. 'From the look of it I believe it will have come from the young couple who tried camping near the old settlement last year and got blown away. They have sent more books for Wee Ruari which will please him.' While she was putting the food on the table she remembered a question she had been going to ask him. 'You were after saying you will not be going to sea tomorrow. Is there some reason for that? I don't see a sign of coarse weather coming. A breath of autumn maybe…?'

'No weather at all,' he interrupted her, 'but there's a very good reason.' She looked at him quizzically. 'Are you fit for a shock?' he asked blithely.

'Fit enough,' she answered, reassured by his light tone.

'Well then, it's because Euan Ally's wanting to go across to Clachan to see his sweetheart,' Jamie announced.

'Euan Ally has a sweetheart in Clachan?' she echoed. 'I've heard nothing of that.'

'Nor will you have heard,' he replied. 'They wish nothing said about it for a whiley.'

'He's gey young, but he's a nice enough laddie,' she allowed. 'What do you know of the lassie?'

'Not much just,' he shrugged. 'She seems right enough and folks say she's a good worker. Good at the spinning too, I'm told.'

'They're planning to marry, I take it?'

'Ay, as soon as they can.'

'Is she any sort of cook?'

'Euan Ally thinks she is or he wouldn't be wanting to marry her, would he? Not after having a good spell of your own cooking.'

'And have they planned where they are going to live?' she asked. 'I take it he intends to go on fishing with you.'

'Aye, we've agreed that.' He sat down and started to take his soup. His bowl was empty, but there was still no sign of Euan Ally.

'He's long enough out in the scullery,' she observed. 'Does he not want food tonight?'

'He's hungry enough, but he's a wee bitty shy.'

'Euan Ally's shy about facing me?' she asked surprised. 'Why ever so?'

'Say no more,' cautioned Jamie as the scullery door opened and Euan Ally came in, sat down at the table, and began to take his food in his usual hearty way.

'My, but that's good,' he declared when he had finished his second helping of bramble pie. 'I've never tasted the like of that before.'

'Did your mother never make a bramble pie?' she asked.

'Ach, no, mother never troubled herself to make fancy things like that,' said Euan Ally. 'She'd maybe boil a few berries and mix them with cream or crowdie if she was expecting the missionary, but she never put a crust to anything. The old man had no liking for such. He only took food that would slip down without he had to chew. He'd got mighty few teeths for chewing anyway and, seeing there was no such thing as an oven that would get hot in the house, the cailleach reckoned he got all he needed.'

Kirsty wasn't surprised. She'd not met many crofter wives who'd bothered or perhaps not even learned to use any cooking equipment other than a pan and a girdle. Even if there were a cooking range with an oven she'd found the oven flues would, through lack of use, be blocked solid with peat ash so that the oven never became more than lukewarm no matter how much the fire was stoked. She herself had never seen her granny use the oven in their own range, which, though it had called itself a 'Modern Mistress', had been used only for drying kindling. Indeed, she had not known it could be used for any other purpose. It wasn't until she had gone to live in the city that she had seen an oven used for cooking. When, under her old employer's tuition, she had become what even she herself allowed to be a passably good cook, she'd found she enjoyed oven cooking. When she had landed on Westisle, to be confronted by a stark though well-swept kitchen where a few damp peats had been smoking sulkily in a range that looked almost hostile in its neglectedness her spirits had quailed. Curiosity, however, had compelled her to investigate what she believed might be blocked flues. It had been a daunting task but she had been proved right; surveying the appetising spread on the wax-cloth-covered table she complimented herself on her perseverance. Indeed, the whole kitchen looked completely different. Not only was the once shabby range shiny, its grate full of glowing peats; the rough wood floor was smoothed with linoleum; the once bare window embellished with pretty curtains; the primitive wooden bench and the upright chairs, plainly fashioned from driftwood, looked almost inviting with their bright cushions. Her presence had certainly made a big difference and she permitted herself a complacent smile. It was still basic when contrasted with city kitchens but it had acquired its own aura of down to earth welcome and, though she planned further improvements, she was happy enough with it.

Jamie rose from his chair. 'There's light enough for getting a rabbit or two. Will we take a gun?'

'Surely!' agreed Euan Ally. 'We might as well just. It'll maybe save time in the morning.' A moment later they were striding off, guns under their arms.

I dare say Euan Ally's wanting to take a couple of rabbits as a present for his sweetheart, Kirsty thought as she cleared away the dishes and poured herself a cup of tea before sitting down beside the fire and opening her letter. It was, as she'd surmised, from the English couple; a very ordinary letter, or at least it began that way, wishing everyone well and bemoaning the bleakness of the suburbs where they lived, but when she'd turned to the second page her brows began to knit in a small frown; gradually her expression grew more and more incredulous. She started to read the whole letter again, nodding her head every now and then as if to make sure she was grasping the full import of its message. She looked up, staring unseeingly before her; the letter slipped from her loose fingers into her lap where it stayed until she moved to pour herself another cup of tea in the hope that it would help settle her mind. The letter had a curiously discomforting effect on her since, after stating they had fallen in love with her island, it went on to propose quite seriously that she should allow them to buy a small plot of land on Westisle near the old settlement and to rebuild one of the abandoned cottages as a holiday home to which they could come each summer and eventually retire to. They would be glad to pay an annual feu duty as they had understood was the custom and they were careful to stress that she would not be involved in any expense. Apart from the stone already on the site or nearby they would be responsible for transporting all the other building materials required and they could perhaps persuade a Clachan builder to come over each summer until the house was habitable. Kirsty found the whole idea fanciful. It was all very well for folks to claim they had fallen in love with the island after spending only a couple of weeks' holiday, possibly in reasonably good weather, which she recalled the young couple had not been fortunate enough to experience, but she was extremely doubtful if they would want to face the severity of the winter gales, the inevitable shortages and the long isolation from the mainland during days or even weeks of stormy weather. It was different for her having been born and bred on an island and thus well accustomed to such disadvantages.

She'd still been at school when the death of her granny, the only mother she had known, had meant her having to leave her island home and go to live in the city with an elderly aunt who had been her only surviving relative apart from Uncle Donny, her granny's only son. But the authorities had classed Uncle Donny as a 'dummy' and decided he must go to a 'home' where he could be properly looked after.

She had at first found city life exciting and bewildering, but it had not been long before she had begun to contrast the dirty streets and hurried people with the freshness and timelessness of the land she had left. Had she not been well inured to accepting all life's little disadvantages she would somehow have contrived to return.

When she had reached her teens and had been considered old enough to go into service it had been arranged for her to start work at Islay, a superior boarding house belonging to a middle-aged widow who would train her to be a cook general. The widow had been exacting, generous enough with her tuition if not with her money, and since Kirsty had never been used to having money of her own she'd been more than content with her position. The widow had been delighted with her pupil, who had quickly developed into an excellent cook and a conscientious and trustworthy general. The situation had continued happily for over twenty years until the widow's health had deteriorated and as a consequence the management of the boarding house had passed into the hands of a couple of avaricious younger relatives who had all too soon revealed that they had scant interest in the place except as a means of extracting money from guests for minimal food and indifferent service, while on the other hand demanding maximum servility from their staff in return for grudgingly paid wages.

For almost two years, mainly through a feeling of loyalty to the widow who had trained and befriended her, she had endured the situation, but with guests becoming distressingly infrequent it had become plain the boarding house was doomed to failure. She had realised the time was coming when she would have to seek a similar position elsewhere. But where? Employment of any kind with keep was scarce and at the age of nearly forty what chance had she when cook generals were reputed to be 'two a penny'? For some time now she had regarded Islay as her home. The worry of her likely predicament had been on her mind for some time when the shy Ruari MacDonald had chanced to book in at Islay for a couple of weeks. She'd guessed as soon as he arrived that he was an Isleman but when, after only the slightest acquaintance, he had written her a note suggesting marriage she had at first been too astonished to take his offer seriously. It was the first proposal of marriage she'd ever received in her life. And much as it had shaken her at the time, it had made her face up to her position, compelling her to at least consider the possible advantages of accepting his proposal. Here was someone offering her a home. Even if she were honest with herself, she knew she had no desire to return to the rigours of island life – shreds of which still lingered in her memory – it was at least an alternative. It would be a hard life after so many years in the city, but it had needed only a few hours of question and discussion before she had made up her mind to accept.

A few days after they had made their vows in front of the minister she had said goodbye to Islay and the city and had accompanied Ruari by train and boat to Westisle, an island which proved to be even more solitary than the one where she had been born and had spent her childhood. And here she was sitting in her own kitchen, in her own house; now the laird and sole proprietor of the island.

Despite its many inconveniences, she had grown to love her island home, cherishing its seclusion, its wild beauty, its tranquillity and its wildlife. Now the letter she had received that evening gave a possible forewarning of encroachment on her contentment. But, after a few minutes' reflection, she recalled how much she had liked the young couple; how much Wee Ruari, her small son, had taken to them; how pleasant relations had been when a gale had wrecked their tent and they had been forced to accept the hospitality of her home. There had been no sign of discord then and indeed she had actually been looking forward to their setting up camp again on the island in the coming spring. But a more permanent arrangement? Could she agree to their request? Her mind was clouded with doubt. She would need to discuss the matter with 'the boys', of course, but she realised she would have liked the opinion of someone nearer her own age. The only person would be Mhairi Jane who lived in Clachan across the Sound. After she had been widowed, Mhairi Jane had become her staunch friend and self-appointed advisor, but recalling her repeated warnings against being alone on the island Kirsty had no doubt as to what the advice would be.

'I've always said you were a right hardy to have come to Westisle in the first place though you had two good men to see you were alright but mho ghaoil, it's not a good thing for a woman to be alone and living with herself,' Mhairi Jane had warned. When Kirsty had pointed out to her that she was not alone for much of the time since the 'two boys' were not out fishing at weekends Mhairi Jane had said, 'What I'm saying is it's not a good thing for a woman to be living day after day by herself; she might get to like it. You could do with some company mho ghoaoil. Why don't you try putting an advertisement in a paper saying you'd provide bed and breakfast for touries?'

Kirsty had shuddered mentally.

'What, on Westisle!' she'd demanded. 'Bed and breakfast could lead to their being stranded by the weather for a week or more. Anyway, I wouldn't want to be washing sheets day after day.'

'Only pillow slips,' Mhairi Jane had argued. 'You'd not be getting tinkers or layabouts here so you'd need only to put the sheets through the mangle just. Kate na Viarry here reckons sheets need to be tubbed no more than once a week no matter how many folks has been sleeping in them.' Seeing Kirsty's raised eyebrows, she'd lapsed into silence for a moment but had then gone on to say earnestly, 'Indeed mho ghaoil I wouldn't want to see you get like old Phemie Mor on Rhuna that got so fond of bein' on her own after her father had been taken suddenly she didn't wish to see anyone just. Not even one of her own kinsfolk. I'm after telling you she would take to the hills and hide herself rather than she would face a single body. The nurse tried to talk her out of it and so did the doctor but she just threw old boots at them when they came near her door. There was no doin' any good for her at all.'

'Poor soul,' Kirsty had commented under her breath.

'It was a poor soul indeed that was found by Murdoch the shepherd in one of the old bothies up the glen, cold and dead under a pile of bracken and old straw, and none the wiser was she for that,' Mhairi Jane had concluded enigmatically.

'Well, if I ever get to the state of hiding away from folks and throwing old boots at them, I could trust "the boys" would soon enough be teasing me out of it,' Kirsty had responded, slanting a mischievous smile at her, but Mhairi Jane had persisted.

'You could maybe break one of your legs out on the moor while they were at sea and no way of letting a body know save for a bit of smoke if you could even light a fire and supposin' the wind was in the right direction.'

'Oh, I daresay I'd manage to crawl back one way or another,' Kirsty had assured her dismissively but there had been no convincing Mhairi Jane that she had no fears about being alone on the island; she might have fears for her son but he would be away at school for much of the time and she was certain she could protect him when he was home. But she knew beyond doubt what Mhairi Jane's advice would be were she to mention the young couple's proposal.

It was in much the same way that 'the boys' reacted when she told them. 'Give them permission,' Jamie said immediately. 'It'll be company for you.' Euan Ally nodded agreement.

'But I'm not sure if I want company too often,' she retorted. 'Chance visitors I like to see but not long stayers.'

37

'Now that Wee Ruari's started school you'll get to feel lonely in the winter,' Jamie reminded her. 'You'll be missing him during the long evenings.'

'That's different,' she objected, but he ignored her.

Euan Ally had gone outside and was busy cleaning the rabbits they'd brought back with them when Jamie said, 'Euan Ally will be taking a couple of rabbits across to his sweetheart and he'd like fine to bring her over to see the island when he comes back, so I'll wait across there during the day and bring Wee Ruari back with me too. There'd be a bed for her for Saturday night and Sunday if she wants to stay just?'

'Of course,' she agreed, a little sceptical that Euan Ally's sweetheart might want to spend a weekend on Westisle. Island girls were generally opposed to spending time on even smaller islands unless there was some prospect of meeting some man of allowable age and eligibility.

Jamie yawned. 'I'll take myself off to my bed then,' he said. 'I'm kind of tired.'

'You'll be here for your porridge in the morning?' she called after him.

'Aye, but we'll be away as soon as we've taken it. Euan Ally's likely to want to make haste so his sweetheart's father hasn't got time to give her a message to go some place that'll keep her out of sight.'

'Doesn't the bodach approve of Euan Ally then?'

'No, he does not. He doesn't want to lose his daughter to a young man who might take her away from the croft.'

She would have liked to question him further but he was obviously tired. A few minutes later, Euan Ally came into the kitchen wiping his hands on a bundle of grass which he then threw outside. 'They're nice plump beasties,' he told her. 'I've hung a couple in the scullery and I'll take the others across to the old bodach in the morning. That'll please him maybe.'

'Oidche mhath,' he called as, taking off his boots, he went through to his bedroom.

'Oidche mhath,' Kirsty replied and, after warming a mug of milk, took herself to her own room.

chapter five

She was up and had a pan of porridge set beside the fire before either of 'the boys' appeared.

'Here's me thinking you would be up with the birds this morning,' she greeted them.

'Ach, it's a spring tide; there's no need to be rushing,' said Jamie, ladling porridge from the pan.

'Any haste will be this evening so as not to get caught by the tide on the way back,' added Euan Ally.

'You'll make sure and collect Wee Ruari from school when you come,' she reminded them.

Jamie flicked her a teasing glance of reproof. 'I doubt he'd let us forget him,' he quipped.

As soon as they left the house she went through to her bedroom to make it ready for Euan Ally's sweetheart. Not until that moment did it dawn on her that she hadn't asked for the lassie's name. She realised she would be giving up her bed to a girl who was more or less a stranger. When Jamie had asked if there would be a bed for Euan Ally's sweetheart over the weekend her reply had been an automatic 'of course', her island upbringing having imbued in her a natural acceptance that there would always be food and a resting place for a stranger. She had thought at the time that she could make herself comfortable on the bench in the kitchen for a couple of nights but now, steeling herself to the knowledge that a few steps along the passage there was an empty room with an empty bed that no one had slept in since her husband had died, she resolutely took the linen from her own bed, made her way there and unlatched the door. Though she had regularly given the room a cursory cleaning she had made herself do it in a deliberately incurious way as if to avoid coming to terms with her grief. Now, however, as her eyes raked the stripped bed, the neatly folded pile of covers the nurse had placed at the foot, and her husband's Bible, which with his spectacles, lay on the table beside the bed, the poignancy of the scene threatened to engulf her. She sat down heavily on the bed, her head in her hands, her eyes closed while a résumé of her life during the last ten years passed through her mind.

She had never known love, nor had she experienced the excitement of a youthful infatuation. Her first brief marriage at the age of nearly forty had been the result of circumstances and the gentle acceptance of each other by a man and a woman; an acceptance which, fortunately, had developed into similarly gentle affection. Though his sudden death had distressed her it had by no means crushed her.

Tragically, during her second marriage, the knowledge of love, perhaps even passion, had remained undiscovered until it had been too late. The shock of her second husband's confession of his love for her only minutes before his last breath, and the revelation of her own love for him had dazed her, leaving her feeling anguished and bereft. The anguish was still acute but time had forced her to accept that it must be consigned to memory as an indulgence she must no longer permit herself. When she raised her head there was a drawn expression on her face but there were no tears. After a few moments she rose and began methodically to cover the bed, which she had never shared, with the linen she had taken from her own. She left the Bible on the table, put the spectacles away in a drawer, and after a brief survey closed the door firmly. Returning to her own room, she began putting fresh linen on the bed ready for Euan Ally's sweetheart.

She was waiting at the shore to welcome them when *The Two Ruaris* (Jamie had considered it unlucky to change the name of the fishing boat) nosed close enough to the landing rock to put Wee Ruari and Euan Ally's sweetheart ashore. Wee Ruari leapt forward eagerly and bounded over the rocks with hardly more than a gesture and a twinkling glance towards his mother.

'Ach, that's the way of it,' Kirsty excused him, smiling a welcome as she shook hands with Euan Ally's sweetheart, a plump lassie with an abundance of dark hair. She guided her over the boulders. 'Racing this way and that way and never stopping for a word between-ways,' she continued. 'I hope he's been good to you while you were on the boat.'

'Oh surely he has indeed,' was the reply. 'I'm hearing he's a fine scholar.'

'Ach, good enough I reckon,' said Kirsty, gratified. 'He was always keen enough to learn.' She led the way to the house. Loath to ask the girl for her name she was hoping she could discover it without a direct question. 'Is it near the schoolhouse your father has his croft?' she asked, trying to steer the conversation in a suitable direction.

'No, no, indeed, it is right at the far end of the bay,' the lassie replied. 'Close to the "Carrie croft" as it is called.'

'I fear I don't know the "Carrie croft",' Kirsty had to admit. 'I've stayed in Clachan only once or twice and except for the few folk who have come over here in the summer I doubt I would have met many of your neighbours.'

'My father came rabbit shooting last year just, and my brothers Tormod and Uisdean came a few times until they left for Oban for the fishing. I fancied coming but my father said I was too young and I must stay and look after my mother, who was known as Katy Vic the weaver, since she could no longer move from her chair without help.'

'Ach then, you are the daughter of Katy Vic that folks reckon is the best weaver in Clachan,' exclaimed Kirsty.

'One of her two daughters,' the lassie admitted proudly. 'Ealasaid, my older sister, went away to be a maid to a rich old lady. She said to me when she left, "Enac mho ghaoil, you must promise me you'll stay and look after our mother since I must earn some money and cannot do that here." So I promised and I stayed beside my mother until she was taken at the back end of last year. So now I must stay and look after my father,' she finished glumly.

Kirsty felt easier now that she had learned the lassie's name. 'So your mother was the weaver,' she said. 'Indeed, I didn't know she'd passed on.'

'She went without pain,' Enac acknowledged.

'And do you yourself do any weaving?' Kirsty asked after a suitable pause.

'Indeed I do but I am not so good as herself.'

'With time, surely you will be,' Kirsty comforted.

As they came in sight of the house Enac paused and clasped her hands, exclaiming, 'This house is fit for a laird right enough.'

'I believe the laird built it for his son but the lad never came back from the war,' Kirsty confirmed. 'It must have been a sad blow indeed for him. He gave up his whole estate and went back to England. Save for this island, which he gave to my late husband's parents in return for their loyal service.'

'I believe he was a good man, although he was English,' said Enac. 'I've always wanted to see more of the island than I see from Clachan. It looks a friendlier kind of place for having no high hills,' she went on. 'Indeed Euan Ally tells me there used to be a settlement of crofters here but they asked the authorities to transfer them to some place where they could earn a better living.'

'I believe that to be true also,' said Kirsty. 'The old settlement is over on the west side of the island. Much the nicer side I reckon. I expect Euan Ally will be for showing it to you.'

They heard voices as 'the boys' came up behind them.

'And you never told me your sweetheart was a daughter of Katy Vic the weaver,' Kirsty accused Euan Ally. 'I would have been proud to have put on my best skirt that is made of tweed woven by her mother if I had known.'

Euan Ally grunted an inaudible comment as both he and Enac flushed with embarrassment.

Jamie put in, 'Ach, there'll be plenty more years to show her your best skirt. Katy Vic's tweed never wears out.'

As they entered the kitchen they were hailed by Wee Ruari who emerged from the hen-house carrying a basket of eggs. 'Five,' he announced. 'How many this morning?' he asked his mother.

'Guess,' she teased but he went to the scullery and counted the eggs in the bowl. 'Seven,' he said with an exultant smile. 'That would be twelve today would it not?' He always earned a few pence from the sale of eggs so he liked to know that the hens were laying well.

'Indeed, that would be the way of it,' Kirsty acknowledged. 'Now go and clean the dirt off your hands before we take our strupak.' He went outside and dragged his hands through the fresh green grass before offering them for approval.

After the meal was over and Euan Ally and Enac had gone off to see a little more of the island, Jamie said, 'Have you been thinking what you'll say to the couple who wrote to you?'

'It's hardly been out of my mind all day,' Kirsty told him. 'I would not like to leave them too long without a letter.'

'Wait then till I tell you what Euan Ally wishes me to tell you,' Jamie said.

'I'm waiting,' she replied. Jamie glanced towards Wee Ruari who seemed to have fallen fast asleep on the bench.

'Euan Ally has no doubt taken Enac to see what she thinks of the old settlement,' he observed.

'Enac did speak of the old place when we were on the way to the house,' Kirsty interrupted. 'Euan Ally had mentioned it to her.'

'Aye, indeed he would have,' said Jamie. 'He's greatly taken with the place and wonders why the folks would want to leave it. Now he and Enac are speaking of getting married he's keen to know what she would think of him doing up one of the houses and them living there. He's been wanting me to ask you if you would think of letting him have a croft thereabouts, big enough for a souming for sheep and one or two cattle and then he could get his Uncle Lachlan Ruag to come over and do up one of the old houses. He reckons it would be handy for the fishing and Enac would set up her mother's loom and do some weaving. He's convinced it would work out pretty well for them.'

'Why didn't he mention this to me himself?' she asked.

'Ach, you know Euan Ally. He's gey shy when it comes to talking about anything to do with himself,' responded Jamie. 'But when he asks you what would you have to say?'

There was a moment or two of silence while she considered her answer. 'What would you say if the question was put to yourself?' she taxed him.

'Me! I'd be keen enough on the idea but then I know Euan Ally pretty well. What would you say to Enac?'

'She seems a nice enough girl,' Kirsty conceded. 'And she looks strong and sensible enough to cope with life here if she has a mind for it.'

'She has a mind for it right enough, if that's what Euan Ally wants. I'm telling you her old man's tryin' to push her into marrying old Murdoch McLeod who has the next croft to his. It's a good-size croft and the bodach reckons the souming's more than twice his own. He thinks he'll get rich running the two crofts so he's mad keen for Enac to marry the old fellow. He tried to get Enac's sister Ealasaid to say she would do it but she got clean away.'

'What does the lassie herself think of the idea?' Kirsty asked.

'Ach, she's dead set against it,' said Jamie, 'and why wouldn't she be? Murdoch's a dirty old bodach just, a salachar they call him with his beard always matted with stale brose. No, Enac wants for her and Euan Ally to get married as soon as they can to stop her father always goring at her.'

'She told me she had to stay home to look after her father since her mother died,' Kirsty said.

Jamie mumbled an oath. 'Her father can marry the red widow who's always giving him wee drams and strupaks whenever she sets eyes on him. She's keen enough to have him,' he finished disdainfully.

'Has the red widow a croft?'

'Right enough she has but it is no more than half the size of old Murdoch's croft. But the widow herself is comely enough even if she has the name of being on the flighty side. She'll do well enough for him.'

'Doesn't it seem odd that almost on the same day we should hear of two very different couples wanting to come and live on Westisle,' Kirsty said. 'It puts me in a bit of a pickle.'

'Euan Ally's had it in mind for some time,' Jamie disclosed.

'I gathered that for myself,' responded Kirsty.

'He'll no doubt give you a wee while to talk to Enac about it and then put it to you tomorrow.'

She frowned. 'I am fearing there would be responsibilities in having other people here on the island. I really should take some time to think about it.'

'You could tell Euan Ally about the English couple and maybe he would help you to make up your mind,' Jamie suggested.

'I'd like fine for you to be here with me when he speaks to me of his plan,' she said. Rousing Wee Ruari she packed him off to his bed.

'I'll be hereabouts,' Jamie promised.

She expected to be pondering the situation much of the night but the hard embrace of the unfamiliar mattress dissuaded her and she slowly drifted into a deeply relaxing slumber.

chapter six

The following morning being the Sabbath, Wee Ruari, as was his custom, placed the Bible on the table as soon as they had finished their porridge, and waited impatiently for his mother to begin the weekly ritual of reading a chapter aloud. Jamie went outside, but Euan Ally and Enac remained in their seats, their heads slightly bowed as if they too were conditioned to the ritual. When the reading was over, Wee Ruari put away the Bible and ran outside. Almost as if it might have been a prearranged signal, Jamie came back into the kitchen.

'Will I away and milk the cow for you this morning?' he offered Kirsty. 'I've filled a sack of hay.'

'Indeed, that will be very welcome,' she allowed, and went to get the milk pail.

'I was thinking me and Enac would come along with you,' suggested Euan Ally. 'We could maybe take another look at the old settlement.'

'Why don't we all go,' suggested Jamie. 'It'll do no harm to have a good look at it. Maybe it'll help you to make up your mind whether you want to do anything with it.'

They called Wee Ruari and set off in the direction of the old settlement, Euan Ally and Jamie exchanging frequent comments as they walked together, Wee Ruari running in front and calling everyone's attention to everything, which he maintained had altered in one way or another during the week he had been away at school. Kirsty and Enac trailed a little in the rear and Kirsty, wanting to hear what Enac might have to say about Euan Ally's plan to move to Westisle once they were wed, felt it was time to broach the subject.

'So you think you would like to live on Westisle once you and Euan Ally are wed?' she queried.

Enac seemed startled momentarily and looked down at her feet before replying.

'Euan Ally has told you we wish to marry?' she asked searchingly.

It was Kirsty's turn to feel embarrassed. Euan Ally had not spoken to her about his plans for marriage. It was Jamie who had made her aware of them and, though she suspected Euan Ally had spurred him to do so, she felt momentarily flustered as she realised she might have revealed what had been meant to be a secret between them. 'Not yet,' she rushed to admit. 'But once Jamie had spoken to me of Euan Ally having a sweetheart who was wanting to visit Westisle I guessed something was afoot; and since island men are not ones for wasting time once they have an idea it needed little enough thinking of.'

Enac smiled. 'We'd like to get married before the potato planting,' she said simply.

'And you would like the idea of a house here on Westisle? You would not find yourself wanting for company?'

'I believe I would be kept too busy to want for company.'

'You would be for bringing over your mother's loom?'

'That is what I would wish to do. My mother was always saying her loom was to be mine from her own mother so my father must not take it away from me.'

'Would he wish to do that?' Kirsty probed.

'My father would not wish me to marry Euan Ally.' The tinge of regret in Enac's tone belied her grim expression. 'Euan Ally would like to run a few sheep on the hill,' she continued, 'and after the first shearing we could perhaps set up my loom. And there is plenty of crotal to be scraped off the rocks here he tells me. I could start gathering it and storing it ready for the dyeing. We found plenty of whelks which I could gather when the tide is right.' She paused and darted a swift glance at Kirsty. 'You will be thinking I am too far ahead with my plans seein' that you have not told us of your own thinking,' she said contritely.

Kirsty only smiled a vague reply since by this time they had reached the settlement where 'the boys' were enthusiastically inspecting one of the ruined houses. She stood for a moment and with a wide gesture that took in the whole of the bay said, 'If I'd been the laird, this is where I would have chosen to build a house for my son rather than over the other side where he *did* build it. See Enac, there is a good well for water near at hand; a fine level beach for hauling up a boat; a burn close at hand for the blanket washing and flat land for planting and sowing and no distance at all for carrying kelp from the shore. Oh indeed, how happy my own granny would have been to have a croft with so many advantages.'

'Indeed, I see that fine,' agreed Enac, 'but the laird would have wanted his son's house to be distant from the houses of his crofters, surely?'

'I believe that would be the way of it,' acknowledged Kirsty ruefully.

They stood gazing down at the bay, Kirsty relishing the sight of the white gulls riding the furrowed water; the diligent oystercatchers patrolling the shore; the customary heron at the mouth of the burn.

'It looks a good enough shore for a boat,' observed Enac unsentimentally. She swung round. 'Would there not be good fishing from the rocks over-by?' she asked, nodding towards the tumbled boulders that partly screened the far end of the shore from the savagery of the periodic east wind. 'Good creagach fishing I'm meaning,' she explained.

'There might be just,' Kirsty agreed. 'You'd best ask "the boys". I, myself, have never been over fond of creagachs so I've not tried my hand at it and I've not encouraged Wee Ruari to come this way without me.'

'Trodhd.' The shout came from Jamie who was beckoning them closer. 'Euan Ally's after thinking it would take his Uncle Lahac no more than a week or two of fine weather to make this place fit enough for a beginning,' he told them. 'Is that not so, Euan Ally?'

'Aye, indeed,' confirmed Euan Ally. 'Once past the New Year and the better weather is here he could come and make a start. We can clear out one of the bunks on the boat so he'll have some place to sleep when we're ashore.'

'Your Uncle Lahac could have part of the empty loft at the house if he'd bring his own bed,' Kirsty surprised herself by offering, aware that she had seemed to have acceded to Euan Ally's request without it having been directly put to her. She caught the glance that was exchanged between Euan Ally and Enac, wordless but easily interpreted. She saw Jamie's expression of approval and experienced a warm feeling of having bestowed a much longed for favour.

'I'd best go and get the cows milked,' said Jamie, picking up the bag of hay and the milk pail from where he had put them. 'Are you for coming with me and we'll take a look at Brechty's udder and see if it's healed rightly?' Kirsty nodded agreement. The sting on Brechty's udder had healed a day or two previously but Jamie must want to speak to her about her thoughts on the settlement, and this was a way he would be sure of her undivided attention.

'So you're going to let Euan Ally take over a croft on Westisle,' he remarked as soon as they were out of earshot. 'I reckon you've done well enough for the island and for yourself,' he added.

'You reckon?' she echoed.

'Aye indeed, Euan Ally will make a fair enough crofter and shepherd and I believe Enac will be a hard-working wife for him.'

They plodded on silently until Kirsty said, 'I'll need to come across with you in the morning when you take Wee Ruari back to school. I will then take the bus to the factor's office. He will tell me what I should do about granting Euan Ally a croft with a fair souming and a fair rent.'

'You're reckoning on seeing him tomorrow?' Jamie seemed surprised.

'Now I'm of a mind I wish to get things settled,' she told him.

'And the English couple? Will you speak to him about the English couple?'

She thought for a moment. 'I believe it might be a good idea,' she allowed.

53

Jamie gave a little chuckle. 'An English couple alongside an island couple,' he chaffed. 'You think they will make a good match.'

She permitted herself a faint smile. 'We shall have to wait and see what they themselves make of it just,' she said.

She was put ashore in Clachan, along with Wee Ruari, the next morning and caught the bus to the factor's office where things were settled with surprising speed. The factor was helpful, though plainly sceptical at the idea of the island becoming repopulated after so many years. He disinterred an ancient map with the area of the old crofts vaguely indicated along with ideas of past soumings and rights of grazing. He also advised her about fair rents, offering to collect them for her annually, as he did for the laird of Clachan. Feeling well reassured she left his office, caught the bus back to Clachan then took the opportunity to call on Mhairi Jane for a strupak and a 'wee crack' while she waited for 'the boys' to collect her and take her back to Westisle. Mhairi Jane's reaction to her news had been entirely as she had expected.

'Ach, mho ghaoil is mhath leam sin,' she had enthused, reverting to the Gaelic in her excitement. Grasping both Kirsty's hands, she shook them feelingly. 'I will be sleeping in my bed the happier for the knowing of it.'

'I'm hoping that it will also make me happy,' Kirsty riposted, a little less enthusiastically.

She and 'the boys' sat until the early hours of the morning looking at the old map the factor had given her.

'They were mighty small crofts in those days,' observed Jamie. 'Euan Ally will need three or four of them to gather

54

enough hay and corn for the cattle and sheep he has in mind.'

'We will work that out between us when we are not so tired,' Kirsty insisted on a half yawn. 'I shall write to the English couple in a day or so and tell them what I have to offer.'

They said their 'Oidhche mhaths' and, rising from her chair, Kirsty went to close the partly open outer door where she stood for a few moments listening intently to the quietness of the night; a quiet so unusual that the softly clear cries of golden plover sounded almost as if the birds were on the roof. She'd always thrilled at the sound of golden plover calling in the dark. They seem to be staying kind of late this year, she reflected.

chapter seven

The news of Euan Ally's plans to take a croft on Westisle brought much unfavourable comment from the Clachan crofters.

'An island that's once been forsaken by crofters is no place to start a new life,' some said, and when it became clear that Euan Ally and Enac planned to get married and live on Westisle the comments became scathing. 'Euan Ally's a right loon to be thinking of taking a young wife over there. She'll never settle in a place that has no company enough for a ceilidh and no post office. Isn't life gey hard for women even here though we have a mail bus twice a week that will take us to the ferry and a post office telephone no more than a mile away. Enac's just as much of a loon to say she'll go with him to my way of thinking.'

Euan Ally was defiant. 'There's safer anchorage for a boat on Westisle than there is hereabouts and the land's no worse for grazing and what's more there'll be a landlord that's likely to be fairer by far than the one you have here,' he told them.

'But you have no church there,' one or two of the more pious pointed out.

'Can we no speak to the Lord under our own roof then the way we have to on the boat?' demanded Euan Ally, but by then they had dismissed him as one of the godless and had shut their minds to his arguments.

Kirsty herself heard little of their criticism. 'They've taken a good look at what I'm offering, and seeing they think it's fair enough they've made up their own minds to it,' was her retort if ever the matter was mentioned in her presence.

'I believe Enac's father will be near off his head when he's told of the arrangements to his face,' chuckled Mhairi Jane impishly. Enac's father was not a well-liked man in Clachan and, much as they might deplore Enac's decision to move to Westisle, there were not a few who looked forward to the pleasure of witnessing the bodach's chagrin when he would at last have to face the fact that he was to lose Enac and the prospect of a large croft, and content himself with taking on the 'red widow' and the smaller croft she would bring him as an alternative.

When Euan Ally had first spoken to his Uncle Lachy about wanting to do up one of the old houses on Westisle his uncle had scoffed at the idea. 'The Dear knows but it's plenty years since those old dwellings have had life in them,' he'd responded. 'Even if there's good stonework still there's not a reed nor a spar of an old roof left.'

Euan Ally was not too disheartened. 'Ach that's the like of the man just,' he confided to Kirsty. 'Always arguing with himself when there's no one else to argue with. I'll have to wait and see just. He'll haver for a while but I believe he has a mind to come over and take a look at what needs to be done. He'll be telling folks how impossible it is at the same time as he's telling himself how much there'd be to do and the time it will take him to do it, and before he goes back to Clachan I doubt he'll be reeling off a list to me and Jamie of all the stuff we'll be needing to bring over for him from the agriculture store on the mainland.'

'Did you say to him that if he cares to do the work there will be room for him to bide up in the loft here at night so long as he will bring some sort of bed for himself to lie on?' Kirsty asked.

'I did indeed!' exclaimed Euan Ally, his hand wiping away the beginnings of a smile. 'An' didn't his wife, that's my auntie Meggie just, near shoot the eyes out of her head with the glare she fastened on him at the idea of it. "No indeed, you'll not bide a night under the same roof as a lone widow," she warned him, so I reckon me and Jamie will have to bring the boat in each night after the fishing so he can have the spare bunk.'

'He'll be wanting me to feed him just the same?' she asked.

'Aye, right enough and I doubt he'll be bringing over young Padruig Mor when he's likely to be needing a hand.'

'Young Padruig Mor?' she queried.

'Aye, him that has the bowed legs and strength of a bull, and the brains of an empty bucket,' said Euan Ally. 'But he's a good worker though he's the most beautiful liar God ever put two boots on. His mother's forever greetin' that he eats as much in a day as would an army in a week.'

'I expect that I'll manage to satisfy him,' Kirsty observed passively.

A short time after Euan Ally's uncle agreeing to come and do the work 'if the Lord spared him', 'the boys' began to bring over some of the materials he required from the crofters' agricultural store. First, however, they had to contrive a shelter sturdy enough to protect these from the weather, and yet to be as near as possible to the settlement. Materials which would be useless if once soaked by rain, Kirsty allowed to be stowed in the loft of her house. It was not an ideal solution since, as not even a wheelbarrow could cope with the rough terrain of the moorland between house and settlement, it would necessitate their having to be transported by means of a hand barrow or, more likely, on the backs of men. It was ever so, Kirsty reminded herself with a sigh, recalling childhood memories of crofters – both men and women – labouring up the brae with full bolls of meal and flour on their backs as well as drums of tar and coils of rope after the bimonthly steamer had unloaded its cargo.

Once all the materials had been brought to the island and stowed and when Uncle Lachy had been informed they were there ready for him, he still delayed his appearance. It was understandable. Euan Ally had reported that once the autumn potato lifting was finished his uncle had started to get himself ready for the New Year celebrations, and after New Year he was needing time to recover from his excesses. He wouldn't be fit for much building for a whiley just, his nephew accepted resignedly. Also, there were two more conditions to be observed in addition to the one forbidding him to sleep beneath the roof of a lone widow, but they were by no means unexpected. When he was not 'on the whisky' as Euan Ally put it, his uncle was a devout man and he must cease work early on a Saturday so as to give him time to prepare himself for the Sabbath and secondly, even though the missionary might not be able to get over to Westisle to keep an occasional eye on him, Lachy must not so much as look at or lay his hands on a tool on the Sabbath day. Euan Ally and Kirsty accepted both conditions as a matter of course. It was Jamie who murmured dryly, 'Clachan folks believe their God is eyeless.'

As always the winter came swiftly, enclosing them with storm-force winds, rain and mountainous seas. The fishing boat *The Two Ruaris*, hauled up safe and snug in her winter berth, was awaiting the coming of spring and calmer weather. Kirsty fretted because she was able to see Wee Ruari only sporadically, it being a matter of snatching, at the most, perhaps an hour of calm between tides when 'the boys' could launch the *Katy* and nip quickly across the Sound to collect or to deliver him home or to school. They refused to allow Kirsty to go with them and she made no attempt at argument knowing full well that, in a sudden squall, a third person plus Wee Ruari would only increase the risk. She had perforce to settle herself as well as she could on the headland overlooking the Sound and wait, her eyes often blinded by spray, her mind racked and her body tensed with the agony of watching as the frail-looking little *Katy* did her best to combat the assault of the uneasy grey sea. Her only respite from watching was when Euan Ally intended staying over in Clachan to see Enac, and Jamie and he would yield to her plea to be allowed to accompany him.

After one such visit to Clachan, Euan Ally brought news that, since the fishing boat was laid up, and his uncle had declared that it would be a whiley before he could start work, he and Enac had decided to make a quick trip to Glasgow where they would be married. Enac's sister, who was a companion to a rich old lady who lived in the city, had written to say that her employer was going to stay with a relative for a time so the couple could be accommodated in the house for the time they needed to be there. Also, the staff would not only be delighted to welcome the new bride and groom but would also be happy to give a little celebration afterwards. So it was arranged that during the next short spell of calm Jamie would ferry Euan Ally over the Sound where he would join Enac for the journey to the city.

Euan Ally had said he wanted to be back on Westisle in good time for the beginning of the fishing season, and since there would be no possibility of their 'but and ben', as Jamie chose to call it, being restored sufficiently to provide even a few vestiges of shelter, Kirsty suggested that they might care to live with her after they were married, taking over her bedroom which she had cleared ready for Enac's weekend visit and had not since reoccupied. It had seemed to her a simple answer to the problem and both Enac and Euan Ally had welcomed the idea. 'Maybe Enac will learn to cook food the way you do yourself,' he'd suggested.

'I'm sure Enac is a fair enough cook without learning anything from me,' she'd demurred.

'Aye, but you cook grand pies with crusts and cakes and puddings and treats. I doubt she'd be up to that.'

'You will need to get yourselves a proper cooking range even better than the one you see here, ' Kirsty informed him. 'She'll not manage those sort of things on a girdle.'

'Aye, she's been looking at pictures of stoves and we hope to take a look at others while we're away. She fancies one that's called a "Modern Mistress". It speaks well for itself, she thinks.'

Kirsty was dubious. Her granny's stove had been a 'Modern Mistress', but of course that had been many years ago.

'Well, you'll need to tell your uncle to be sure and fit a chimney on your house. I doubt if any stove you would buy nowadays would suit a hole in the roof to let out the smoke as there would have been in the bothies at the old settlement.'

'Aye, and doesn't he know that fine. Wasn't it his own father just that put on a good many of the tiled roofs with chimneys in Clachan and never a one to this day has been taken away by the storms. Aye indeed, Uncle Lachy is said to be a grand chimney man himself,' claimed Euan Ally.

It was arranged that when the bridal couple wished to return to Westisle they would make a fire with plenty of smoke on the cliff above the Clachan schoolhouse and, as soon as there was a spell of calm, Jamie would go across to meet them and ferry them over. Kirsty busied herself baking a fruit cake with a good sugar coating which she put away in a cupboard where neither Wee Ruari nor Jamie would be likely to see it, for they would almost certainly take a slice from it. That done she made sure that her old bedroom was completely ready to receive the young couple; mused upon what alterations, if any, she would be wise to make before sharing her home and her kitchen with another woman, and then composed herself to carrying on with her ordinary winter lifestyle.

With the fishing boat safely ashore Jamie had, without the slightest hint from her, taken over the responsibility of feeding and milking the cattle. She was extremely grateful that she did not have to face the daily trudge in all weathers over the moors. Whenever he could make the time Jamie would go over to the settlement to 'sort' the stonework in readiness for Euan Ally's uncle to begin work when he did eventually come over. She never knew how he 'sorted' the stonework but accepted that he was being helpful. Back at the house he was equally helpful, always ensuring that the peat buckets were full, thus saving her the burden of carrying them, and cutting plenty of kindling. He's a right good laddie she reflected, accepting that his childhood had probably been lacking in warmth and wondering if, at any time in his life, any adult had shown or spoken to him of affection. It seemed improbable from what she had learned and he himself had never spoken of having fond memories of anyone from the past. He had appeared touched by his father's death but apparently no more so than when his uncle had died, though she accepted that any sign of emotion would have been masked by the bluff practicality that deflected all solace. And yet he's a warm-hearted boy, Kirsty conceded. There was no doubting the affection that existed between himself and Wee Ruari, and he and Euan Ally were staunch friends; unlike Euan Ally, however, he had shown no interest in any of the Clachan lassies who had visited the island infrequently during the summer months. Despite his physique, his fearless blue eyes, his dark good looks and his unruly black hair, she had to allow that the indifference appeared mutual but that, she had assumed, was because in Presbyterian Clachan Jamie was still regarded as a Papist. She was sure the day would come when he would fall for some nice lassie who would genuinely return his interest.

When that day comes, she told herself, the lassie will have got herself the chance of a grand husband. She wondered if Euan Ally's forthcoming wedding had perhaps slanted Jamie's ideas in that direction but knew only too well that she would be given no inkling of such a happening until all was settled between himself and his chosen one.

She began to wonder if it might be kind to indicate that she had grown to think of him not simply as her stepson but as a true son and to assure him, if such assurance was needed, that he, or indeed he and any bride of his, would never lack a welcome in her home. The more she thought over it the firmer became her conviction that it would be the right thing for her to do. One noisy evening, as the storm was howling and bustling round the house and the hailstones rat-tatting at the windows, he came indoors carrying two overfull pails of peats and a bundle of kindling. Kirsty burst out in a sudden surge of gratitude, 'Jamie, you know you're as good as a son to me. I'll always be fond of you and be grateful to you for the help you've given me.'

He put down the buckets by the hearth and kicked them roughly into position. Straightening up he glared angrily above her head. 'Stop talking bloody nonsense, woman,' he admonished her and, pulling his oilskin more firmly about him, he stumped back outside preferring to face the elements. She flinched. He had never before addressed her so harshly, yet she could not regret having spoken.

chapter eight

The winter had been harsh, the storms starting early and bringing unusually heavy snow which had lingered chillingly into a belated spring. At the end of April, Westisle still had a stark look about it as if not yet recovered from the mauling of the weather, while across the Sound the stately hilltops above Clachan were still capped by winter-white bonnets above black skirts that were becoming burnished by melting snow and liberally scored by silvery burns rushing and tumbling to join the swollen rivers and shadowed lochs.

Wee Ruari had not managed to make it home for Halloween and, in his absence, Kirsty had mused over distant memories of the festivals held in her young days when her granny was still alive; the secret excitement of the evenings, prior to the festival, that had been devoted to mask-making; the thrill of seeing her granny's pretended fright when Kirsty had confronted her wearing the finished article; Uncle Donny's good-humoured grumbling that his bed in the loft took a long time to settle after she had rooted amongst the old clothes of which it was mostly comprised. It had been so much fun on the night, dressing up and donning their masks before joining the other children with much giggling as they revealed their identities; lighting the lanterns which had been patiently hollowed out from the biggest turnip that could be found in the winter store and then trooping off together to indulge in a night of merry mischief-making. Hammering on doors, they would challenge the occupants to guess their identities. Almost always they would be rewarded with a piece of scone and jam, or maybe a softened biscuit from a treasured tin, unearthed from beneath a recess bed where it had probably been secreted since the previous Halloween. Whatever the reward, the children were always delighted with it.

Where doors had remained closed they would retaliate by stealthily removing some piece of equipment lying around, such as a cherished and easily identifiable peat iron, which might be found the next day buried in a neighbour's peat stack; a cas chrom might be hidden behind the barn; a wheel-barrow deposited half a mile away. When their lanterns had burned out the children usually spent the rest of the night spying on the more adult pranksters who, not being so much in fear of a skelping, dared to go further with their mischief. They would pile peats on top of some old groucher's chimney so that, coughing and retching from the smoke, he would have to fling open the door and come outside to be jeered at while the house cleared of peat reek, or maybe they would strike matches and throw them onto some old bodach's reed roof.

There was never any malice in the tricks played by the children or by the more adult pranksters – just a reckless desire to tease. No danger was envisaged since the perpetrators reckoned on being near at hand, ready to rally round and help should the situation show the least sign of becoming threatening. 'Ach, it was all good fun,' they would intone the next morning and the victims, no doubt mindful of their own youthful misdemeanours, knew that they were expected to nod tolerantly and murmur dismissively, 'Aye, right enough and Halloween comes but once a year just.'

No, Kirsty reflected, Wee Ruari would have been only too happy to have stayed in Clachan for Halloween. He would have had much more fun.

Euan Ally and Enac had planned to return to Westisle within a week or two after they had departed for their wedding and honeymoon, but two months had passed and there had been no visible smoke signal to indicate that they were waiting to be picked up from Clachan. Meanwhile, Jamie and Kirsty, after inspecting this year's proposed potato plot, decided conditions were right and it was high time to begin planting. Jamie brought out the heavy cas chrom from the shed where it had spent the winter and began the ploughing while Kirsty, a poc of seed potatoes hanging from one hip and a poc of manure from the other, followed behind him dropping a handful of dung and a potato at regular intervals into the furrow. The task brought back vivid memories of her childhood on her granny's croft when it had been her Uncle Donny wielding the cas chrom and her granny following behind manuring and planting in exactly the same way as she herself was now doing. She'd been too young then to be trusted with the actual planting and her job had been simply to follow along the furrow and kick back the turves to cover the potatoes.

About a third of the plot had been planted when Jamie paused and, supporting himself against the cas chrom, peered with narrowed eyes across the Sound. 'See that now,' he instructed. 'I reckon that must be the pair of them wanting back.'

Kirsty straightened and followed his gaze. The drift of smoke above the schoolhouse was scarcely distinguishable from the lowering cloud. 'Ach, it is so,' she agreed, flexing her stiff shoulders and massaging her aching back. 'I believe that's them right enough.'

'I'd best away and get the *Katy* then,' said Jamie, carrying the cas chrom underarm and setting it against the earth dyke that bounded the plot. 'That will take no harm for a whiley,' he added kicking the earth from his boots.

'Do you see the rain on its way?' Kirsty asked, discerning the assemblage of thin grey mist that was beginning to lower itself over the hills.

Jamie followed her gaze. 'I'd say it's likely enough,' he admitted.

'I was wanting it to stay away until the dark.' There was only a tinge of regret in Kirsty's voice. 'But I reckon I'll be glad enough of a wee rest from my labours. These days my back gets stiff with too much bending.' She detached the two sacks and untied the rope from around her waist before taking them to the shed. 'I reckon I could as well be making a wee strupak for the wanderers.' She spoke as if the thought had just entered her head, though it had smote her with relief the instant she had seen the smoke.

'I'm away then,' Jamie called as he strode down to where the *Katy* was moored.

Kirsty rested for a moment and then stooped to draw her dung-caked hands several times through the clean moist grass before going back to the house.

In the kitchen she kicked off her earthy boots, replaced her rough sack apron with a clean cotton one and set to work preparing what she had spoken of as a 'wee strupak', though she knew it must be something more satisfying. She baked fresh girdle scones, and boiled a pan of salt herring and a pan of potatoes – a meal which she knew from her own experience and from oft-repeated appreciation was accepted as the fare all islanders yearned to return to when they were away from home. Finally she set fresh butter and crowdie and cream on the table. She pondered putting out the cake she had baked in readiness for the return of the newlyweds but, deciding it would be best left until Wee Ruari was at home so he should not be excluded from any celebration there might be, she left it in the cupboard. After setting fresh peats on the fire she set about mixing the hens' mash, thinking she would feed them earlier than customary. This would leave herself time to take the binoculars down to a spot where she could overlook the Sound and watch for the return of the *Katy*. However, on taking out the mash she saw to her dismay that the mist she had noticed earlier veiling the hills had by now drifted so close that it was shrouding the whole Sound. There would be little chance of noticing a small boat like the *Katy*, and even the noise of her outboard motor would likely be either muffled or deflected.

The check to her plans brought the realisation that she was now actually genuinely looking forward to the return of Euan Ally and Enac. Hitherto her feelings had settled into what had become little more than a resigned acceptance of their residence in her home; a necessity which must be endured at least for the time being. Had she, she asked herself, grown to cherish her privacy too much? Had Mhairi Jane been right to chide her on her preference for being alone? She leaned back in her chair, staring at the changing patterns of the glowing peats, her mind wrestling with her confusion, until the sound of thudding boots and voices reached her through the open door.

There were warm and hearty greetings and exclamations followed by Euan Ally and Enac retailing their experiences and impressions of Glasgow. They were almost too excited to eat as they told how they had travelled on tram cars; had twice visited a cinema; had been to a theatre and had attended a roup. Enac enthused about the splendid shops and the outdoor markets she had seen and Euan Ally boasted of having been to a billiard-hall and a funeral. And yes, of course, they'd inspected several cooking ranges and had chosen one which both Enac's sister and the cook at the rich old lady's house had recommended as being suitable. The range was, they said, to be put on the very next steamer to be calling at the nearest mainland port and then to be shipped to Westisle, along with a dresser and a purple and gold pottery clock which they had bought at the roup.

'A clock?' queried Kirsty. 'Does it give the time?'

'Not so that you'd notice,' said Euan Ally with a grin. 'But Enac was that taken with it.'

'It will look grand on the dresser,' Enac defended. 'And who needs the time anyway?'

'No one on this island,' approved Kirsty.

'And while we were in Clachan we arranged for my loom to come over as soon as Jamie and Euan Ally have *The Two Ruaris* sorted,' Enac told them delightedly. 'You *will* make room for it?' she appealed to Kirsty.

'In the shed where we keep the cas chrom. I should think we will be well finished with the potato planting before your loom arrives.'

'Did you not bring a wee present for herself from Glasgow?' Euan Ally reminded Enac.

'Indeed I did,' she responded. 'It's there in one of the boxes just inside the door.' Euan Ally brought in a small box which he dumped on the table. Enac lifted out a brown paper-wrapped parcel which she placed in front of Kirsty. 'That's for you,' she announced impressively. As soon as she touched the parcel Kirsty guessed what it contained.

'Well, isn't that beautiful just!' she exclaimed as she unwrapped the large loaf of city bread. 'If I hadn't already eaten my fill I would be wanting to taste a piece of it at this very moment.'

'Will you not do that, surely?' Enac's tone expressed her disappointment. 'I got it from a good baker,' she insisted. 'I thought it would do as a kind of wedding cake.'

'Well then, if the three of you will join me,' Kirsty yielded, relieved that she had decided not to put out the celebration cake she had made for the occasion. Taking a sharp knife from the table drawer she cut four thick slices. The loaf felt hard and the crust was black. She was glad there was plenty of butter on the table.

When, in her teens, she had first been given city bread Kirsty had thought it tasted like cake, and had declared she would be happy to make a meal of it. The daily visit to the bakery with its racks of fresh-smelling, crusty bread had become for her one of the small delights of the city, though it had not lessened her appetite for the girdle-baked scones and bannocks which had been her childhood fare. Since she had lived on Westisle the smell and taste of city bread had, of necessity, become a remembered experience. Now, biting into her lavishly buttered slice she was more than disillusioned.

'It's got a bit stale, hasn't it?' observed Enac apologetically. 'I got it only the day before the Sabbath thinking since we were to be leaving early on the Monday morning I might not be able to catch the baker.'

'It's still good,' championed Euan Ally with his mouth stuffed so full the butter was oozing down his chin. 'Would you not say so Jamie?'

'It's no bad,' Jamie mumbled thickly, after taking a gulp of tea. A comment of 'no bad' from Jamie could be interpreted as high praise or polite disapproval. He rarely committed himself. Kirsty nodded prudently as she chewed her last mouthful. She estimated from Enac's account that the loaf was likely to be at least five days old and, reckoning she could safely secrete the rest of the loaf in the hens' mash bucket the next morning, she rose and began to clear the table.

'We started the potato planting today,' Jamie told Euan Ally.

'You did? With the cas chrom?'

'Aye, we did so.'

'The land's right enough for the cas chrom then?' Euan Ally sounded a trifle unsure.

'It's right enough. We plan to finish tomorrow if the rain will stay away,' said Jamie.

'I'll give you a turn with the cas chrom then, and maybe we'll start planting my own potatoes before the end of the week,' Euan Ally proposed. 'Enac will give us a hand, if she's a mind.'

'I don't see why not,' agreed Jamie. He nodded in Kirsty's direction. 'No doubt herself wouldn't say no to you giving her a spell or two.'

'I'm ready to give you more than a spell,' Enac volunteered eagerly. She turned to smile fondly at Euan Ally. 'Did we not say we would wish to be married before the time for the potato planting?'

'We did indeed,' he confirmed. 'And there'll be much to do still. We've to get the peats cut and carried without wasting any more time. We've brought a peat iron with us so we'll be kept busy enough. We can be ready to start working at the peats once we've got the potatoes in the ground.'

'I'll be more than ready,' Enac told him.

'And we'll need to have *The Two Ruaris* ready for sea by the spring tide,' Jamie reminded them.

'And the fo'csle dried out ready for when my uncle comes,' added Euan Ally. 'My, but the days could do with stretching into weeks for the work we need to get done.'

'You're keen enough to start?' Jamie eyed him sharply as if uncertain of his willingness to resume fishing now that he had a wife.

'Amn't I keen,' responded Euan Ally fervently. 'The fish have had a long enough rest.' He yawned loudly and, standing up, looked at Kirsty with arch enquiry.

'Everything is in order for you,' she assured him, nodding briefly in the direction of the passageway.

'Then come you along to our bed,' he urged, pulling an unresisting Enac up from her chair and shepherding her in front of him. 'Oidhche mhath.' There were giggles as the door closed behind them.

The morning dawned quiet, still shrouded in mist, but mist could not be allowed to delay the potato planting and, as soon as they had taken their porridge, all four of them were ready to start work. Euan Ally said, 'Seein' there's four of us we would be the better for two cas chroms would we not?'

'There's never been more than one cas chrom on the island,' Kirsty told him. 'Not that I've ever seen.'

'Surely there's no need for the four of us then,' he pointed out. 'If Jamie will plough the first of the furrows, I will plant and manure behind him and Enac can follow me and turn the turves. I will then take a turn at ploughing a furrow and Jamie will see to the planting. Will that not be the best way of it? We could be finished before midday likely?'

'Likely enough,' Jamie acknowledged with a nod.

'And will Enac be keen enough to kick back all the turves herself?' queried Kirsty, unwilling to accept that she was in effect being dismissed from doing what she regarded as her rightful share of the labours.

'Surely,' countered Enac with a broad smile. 'Have I not been given that task since my legs were strong enough to kick?'

'If that's to be the way of it then I'll away back to the house and maybe do a little flannel washing,' Kirsty submitted. Enac shot her a cryptic glance. The lassie's probably never heard of 'doing a little flannel washing', Kirsty excused her, recalling Mrs Ross, her erstwhile employer at the boarding house, telling her that, in her experience, ladies interviewing girls for prospective servants always made a point of asking, 'And can you do a little flannel washing my dear?' The question had struck them both as being somewhat quaint and subsequently whenever there might be a slight gap in the day's programme the expression 'I can always do a little flannel washing' had been exchanged between them. I'll have to explain to Enac sometime, Kirsty thought, that in those days it was customary for ladies to wear flannel petticoats.

When she got back to the house she decided it would be a good idea to do some washing despite there being little prospect of drying anything while the mist stayed as low as it was. She got out the washboard, ran hot water from the range boiler into the tub and began to scrub some towels. When she took them to lay out on the dyke to dry she saw the mist was already being routed by a brisk wind, which was also bringing the sounds of frivolous banter and laughter from the direction of the potato plot. A feeling of disquiet affected her momentarily.

'They think I'm too old to join in their fun,' she told herself, 'and maybe they're right at that. I'm near thirty years past their age and no doubt they will have seen changes and read things in newspapers and magazines that I would never have set eyes on.' Yet she didn't feel old enough to accept being thought of as getting old, she encouraged herself. She was still fit and strong. 'I'll have to try and learn the new ways just,' she thought.

There came a shout and looking up she realised they had seen her and were calling to her to, 'put the kettle on the fire for a strupak, seeing we're near finished.' Raising one of the towels she waved an acknowledgement and made her way quickly back to the house. By the time they were stamping their muddy boots outside the door she had fresh scones and oatcakes ready for them.

The following day they ploughed and planted Euan Ally's potato plot.

'Will the weather be fit to get across for Wee Ruari tomorrow, you reckon?' Kirsty asked, anxiously appraising the portents of the skeletal fingers of white cloud that were stretching across the sky. She'd become much more studious of weather prospects since her son had been going to school and though she had, from earliest childhood, imbibed sky- watching and weather lore as naturally as she had imbibed all other learning, her years in the confines of the city, where one rarely glimpsed more than a segment of sky, had dulled her awareness.

'I doubt there's likely to be any wind to speak of,' soothed Jamie after a brief glance. 'Me and Euan Ally are aiming to get across in *Katy* at first light, since he's keen to talk to his uncle about coming across to start work on his house. We'll keep an eye on the weather and if there starts to be a wild look about it we'll go to the schoolhouse and see will the dominie let Wee Ruari come before the end of his day's schooling?'

She nodded her agreement. The dominie was known to be strict about school hours, but his own good reports on her son's scholastic progress coupled with his under-standing of the uncertainty of getting him home at weekends would, she had little doubt, urge him to consent. Probably he would salve any scruples of conscience he might have by giving Wee Ruari an extra lesson or two to do at home she surmised.

As planned, Jamie and Euan Ally and Enac were away in *Katy* shortly after first light the next morning. A lisping wind was bringing rain so fine as to be almost imperceptible; as the boat left the shore the constant ripples of the Sound, though lively enough, were in no way menacing. Kirsty relaxed, quietly confident of seeing her son that evening. She resolved that when she returned from the milking she would set about loosening the winter-packed earth in the small garden at the sheltered end of the house where in previous years she had experimented with growing a few vegetables such as turnips and carrots; crops sturdy enough to withstand the ravages of the summer gales which, though not as annihilating as the autumn and winter gales, could frequently be merciless to anything that could be classed as being the least bit tender. She had once or twice tried to grow cabbages, only to see them being shrivelled or torn bodily out of the ground by the wind when they'd been barely more than tiny rosettes of green. She'd fancied growing flowers such as those she had in the past seen in city parks and suburban gardens. She'd even ordered from a catalogue packets of seed which were described as being 'hardy', but up to date her only reward had been to witness an all too brief blooming of a few flowers that might have born a slight resemblance to the marigolds depicted on one of the packets, before the wind had reduced them to almost leafless and disabled stems. Even that modicum of success had heartened her and she'd rushed outside to gather the tattered remnants of gold that were still visible. Taking them into the kitchen she'd put them into an old tin measure of water, retrieved the paint box and brushes which the English couple had sent Wee Ruari for his birthday and had set to work. She had no skill at painting but the rough outcome had given her a transient satisfaction, if not pleasure. Apart from herself, no one but Wee Ruari had been allowed to see her effort, or so she had believed until the day she had sorted the books in the chest in her late husband's bedroom and the painting had fallen from between the pages of his Gaelic Bible. For a few moments she had been transfixed by the discovery, her breath quickening as she tried to quell the rising torment of her thoughts. How had it come to be there...? And why...?why...? She'd made herself assume that her son, perhaps being childishly proud of her work, had covertly extracted the painting from its hideaway in her drawer; had shown it to his uncle and had then promptly forgotten its existence. Why it had now come to light between the pages of her husband's much revered bible had not been so easy to guess. Fearful of slipping back into the all too easy habit of heartache she had resisted further conjecture, and with tremulous fingers had reinserted the picture, not knowing why she did so. With a corner of her apron she'd wiped away the tears that had filled her eyes and, closing the Bible firmly had replaced it on the chest.

She recalled now as she turned the earth with her graip that there'd been a letter from the English couple in the last post she'd received and, as always, there'd been a postscript plea to allow them to do her a small favour by letting them know of any small items she might be unable to get and might like them to send by post. Up to now she'd baulked at becoming what she thought of as 'too beholden', and pride had made her too reluctant to admit there might be things she would like but which were too difficult to obtain. Resolving that pride must be overcome she determined to add a little postscript to her own letter asking if they would kindly get her a packet of marigold seeds. It would give the young couple so much pleasure to comply with her request, she excused herself as she put the graip back in the shed, and it would cost them very little.

chapter nine

It was late afternoon and the wind was beginning to strengthen with the rising tide; the ripples of the Sound were growing increasingly skittish, showing occasional glimpses of white foam. Kirsty, edgily watching for the return of the *Katy*, was at length rewarded by the sight of a spray-screened shape heading purposefully towards the island. Less than half an hour later her son, his satchel of books swinging from one arm, was racing up from the shore. She always liked to get back to the house before he arrived so that he should not suspect her of watching too keenly for his return. Her anxiety would have embarrassed him.

She was in the kitchen when he burst in; his sou'wester had been blown or pushed back over his shoulder; his hair was tight curled by spray and his face looked in imminent danger of igniting.

'Jamie's brought you something,' he announced, flinging his satchel onto the bench.

'What sort of something?' It was the reply he was expecting.

'You'll need to wait and see what.' His smile was impish.

'I'll do that.' She pulled a towel down from the rack and handed it to him to wipe his face and hair. 'You've brought the sea into the house with you,' she accused him lightly. 'It was kind of coarse?'

After a cursory rub of his head he threw the towel down on top of the satchel, his eyes focusing expectantly on the pile of scones she was buttering. 'It was a bit rockly,' he admitted loftily. 'But that's the way me and Jamie and Ally like it best.' Wee Ruari liked to believe he was already an intrepid mariner.

She pushed a buttered scone along the table towards him.

'Jamie let me take the tiller for a whiley an' we hit a good few lumps before Enac started gurning.' There came the sound of voices from outside and he whispered, 'I reckon Enac's not so good in a boat as she likes to make out.'

Kirsty gave him a sternly reproving glance as Enac came into the kitchen. Her face was fiery but she was flapping her arms to keep warm. 'Oh for a good hot strupak,' she cried as she divested herself of an old oilskin which she had been wearing over her own waterproof.

Kirsty poured her a mug of tea. 'A bumpy crossing was it?' she enquired.

'Bumpy enough, but it's my poor feets that took the cold while I was waiting for Ally to get away from his uncle.' She took a scone and sat down at the bench. 'That old Bheinn Martin saw I was waiting and came over to make me listen to how her cow died at the back end of the year from a spell an old witch had put on it. I've heard the story plenty times before but she went on and on girnin' about losing the best cow she'd ever had that gave milk that was as creamy as butter. She was crouched there on the dyke and

81

she'd taken off her own boots because her corns was killin' her feets, she says, and there she was moanin' about the old witch and her old corns and not seeming put out by the cold. I swear my own feets were that wet just, they got colder and colder hearing her.'

Kirsty smiled. 'Aye, I believe Bheinn Martin makes a right comic of herself once she can find a listener,' she sympathised.

Jamie, coming in, dumped a large cloth-wrapped bundle on the table. 'That's from the wife of Euan Ally's uncle,' he explained. 'She was saying it will help feed him when he gets here and Euan Ally himself is bringing a fine salmon that his uncle landed only last evening.'

'Poached of course,' Kirsty murmured, more by way of an observation than a question.

'Aye, right enough. Over at the Struan. What would you expect?'

At that moment Euan Ally came into the kitchen. He appeared to be struggling to retrieve a large salmon from beneath his rather tight jersey. 'God! You'd think the beast still had life in him,' he exulted, laying the fish proudly on the table. 'Now is anyone going to say that's not a right royal fish?' he demanded and waited impatiently for the expected commendations.

Enac looked at him approvingly. 'But Ally, you didn't say a word to me that you got a salmon from your uncle as well as a haunch of venison from your aunt!' she reproached him saucily.

'No, I did not then,' taunted Euan Ally. 'Why would I be for telling you that one of my family helps himself to the laird's stock whenever he gets the chance? That was always kept a secret.'

'But there's never been a secret about your Uncle Lachy being the best poacher in Clachan and beyond as well as being the best precentor in these parts. Venison, salmon, trout, whatever; there's said never to be a want of such in your uncle's house. I've known that since I was a wee lassie.' Her tone was edged with reverence.

'I believe that's true,' admitted Euan Ally complacently.

'And yet your aunt is so much in fear of the Devil and the missionary, she's dead scared of allowing her man to even put his eyes on a tool hours before the Sabbath let alone on the Sabbath itself,' interjected Kirsty with spurious condemnation. 'Folk respect her for being Godfearing and pious yet you are saying she doesn't care that her man's a regular poacher?'

'No, indeed she doesn't,' Euan Ally affirmed bluntly. 'I believe she's more proud of his poaching than she is of his precenting or anything else he gets up to.'

Euan Ally's admission came as no surprise to Kirsty. A child of the islands, she was not unaware of the anomalies of the religion. There would, of course, be an explanation. She waited while Euan Ally took several gulps of tea. 'See now, this is the way of it,' he proceeded to enlighten her. 'My aunt reckons it's there in the Good Book that the Lord gives to every man five talents and he'll get a greater reward in Heaven if he makes use of every single one of them the best way he can. She reckons if one of her man's talents is to be a good poacher then seein' it's a God-given gift it would be a kind of sin to waste it.'

There was a moment or two of silence before Enac scoffed, 'And yet your aunt's the bold one! Always making so much of the laird's old mother when she calls maybe to give her a piece of venison that her own dogs won't eat!'

'Ach no. That's not the way of it at all. My aunt quite likes the old woman,' Euan Ally defended. 'I believe the old woman carries a copy of the Good Book about with her, and they read it together sometimes, though my aunt doesn't take much of it in since she's more used to a Gaelic Bible.'

There were slightly raised eyebrows but no comments while Kirsty unwrapped and inspected the haunch of venison.

'Will I take that and hang it in the cool?' Jamie volunteered.

'You do that and we'll eat the salmon tonight, unless you would sooner have salt herring again?'

'Salt herring for me,' piped up Wee Ruari.

'And for me and for Ally I expect.' Enac glanced up at her husband.

'Aye, keep the salmon till Monday, till my uncle gets here. He says we're to fetch him then if the weather is good enough,' Euan Ally said.

'You're expecting him to come as soon as Monday?' Kirsty was surprised.

'That's if the Lord spares him,' said Jamie, reminding them that Uncle Lachy never left the Lord out of his calculations. 'He seems keen enough to start now he reckons the worst of the weather's past. Anyway, the laird's taken on a new gamekeeper so he'll be wanting to stay out of the way for a whiley till he hears what like of man he is. The last one kind of winked an eye at Lachy's poaching though well he knew of it.'

'What happened to the last keeper,' Kirsty enquired.

'Ach, hasn't he buggered off, after some woman they're saying,' Jamie observed derisively.

They ate their meal of salt herring and potatoes, and afterwards Kirsty produced the cake she had baked, now resplendent with icing, in readiness for the return of the newlyweds. Their eyes widened in surprise as she put it on the table.

'My, but it's good!' Enac complimented her when she'd taken a bite. 'Better than the one we had in Glasgow. Is that not so, Ally?' Euan Ally nodded enthusiastically, his mouth too full to speak.

'If they make cakes half as good as this in Glasgow then I'm thinking I'd best be away there sometime,' Jamie muttered appreciatively.

'I believe it would be better for a dram of whisky on it,' said Euan Ally, reaching to cut himself another slice. Kirsty forbore from mentioning that the cake had at least one dram of whisky in it.

'It's not as good as clootie dumpling,' stated Wee Ruari flatly. He stood up. 'I'd best go and see if there's any eggs,' he told them, running outside with the egg basket. There would be eggs, Kirsty knew. She always left the laying boxes uncleared when he was likely to be home.

'Look at that!' ejaculated Jamie. 'He's eaten only the icing.' He helped himself to the cake left on Wee Ruari's plate. 'I'll not see it wasted,' he added.

'So your uncle is sure he's seeing signs of the spring?' Kirsty enquired.

'Aye, and he's pretty good at telling the weather.'

'Another of his talents?' she quipped lightly.

'He's right enough there,' put in Jamie. 'I was seeing my first spider this morning just.' He looked at Euan Ally. 'We'll be needin' to get *The Two Ruaris* fit for sea before the weekend.'

'Aye, and dry out the fo'csle for my Uncle has a mind to sleep there when he comes over,' Euan Ally reminded him.

'But can't he sleep in the loft?' Enac protested. 'Kirsty is after putting a mattress up there ready.'

'His uncle's wife forbids her man to sleep in the house when I am here,' Kirsty told her. 'The mattress in the loft was not put there for Euan Ally's uncle.'

'My aunt is feared of Kirsty enticing her man,' explained Euan Ally. Kirsty only smiled.

Enac said, 'Aye, right enough, there'd be plenty of women in Clachan itself would like fine to poach a poacher without him coming here.'

They were still chuckling as Kirsty went out to feed the hens. When she came back Jamie imparted the news that Peggy up at the Cam in Clachan had got 'touries' already, and that Willie Joe had got himself a new boat and was starting to take the 'touries' on fishing trips.

'They're starting early enough,' Kirsty commented.

'Aye, and there's one or two of the wifies has got blankets out on the dykes so they must be expecting more,' Euan Ally confirmed.

'Touries or pilgrims,' Enac supplied. 'First comes the spiders spinning their webs and then come the pilgrims spinning their tales about the best ways of getting to Heaven and then come the tinkers wanting to sell us pails and dippers more than we need, and clothes and towels and things from their bundles.'

'All things in their season,' remarked Jamie quietly.

Ignoring him Enac went on. 'Myself I'd sooner the tinks than any of them, though there's some that steal our peats.'

'Ach, there's few of them do that,' Euan Ally corrected her. 'And I reckon it's worth a few peats to hear the news the tinks bring. They tell us more about what's going on than the newspapers, supposing we could get newspapers here more than once in a whiley anyway.'

'Maybe, maybe,' Enac allowed. 'Though only last spring my own father reckoned they'd lifted a good cartload from his stack on the moors.'

'Ach, your father was always blaming folks for taking peats he'd never cut and lambs he'd counted double,' derided Euan Ally. 'Amn't I blamed for stealing his daughter just?'

'If the tinkers don't steal peats, how do they keep warm,' Enac countered. 'They don't cut them.'

'Ach, with whisky and rough language. When they've taken a few drams, it makes my ears hot to hear them,' answered Euan Ally.

Jamie said, 'Speaking of touries, I've been asked to bring over some fellow from foreign parts that's staying at Mhairi Jane's with his daughter. He's a professor or something like that and his daughter's training to be a botanist whatever that is. They're keen to come to Westisle anyway, so likely if it's calm enough I could collect them on Monday when I take Wee Ruari back to the school and bring them over with Lachy.'

'I must try and be ready for visitors then,' Kirsty acknowledged, and was surprised how much the prospect pleased her.

When *The Two Ruaris* crossed to Clachan on the Monday morning, taking Wee Ruari back to school and returning as expected with Euan Ally's Uncle Lachy, Kirsty saw there were two extra figures aboard. She was too busy making a potach for the milk cow to take much interest but Jamie would, no doubt, bring any visitors up to the house for a strupak and she would meet them then. However, after setting them ashore he seemed to be leaving them to their own devices.

'Ach, they wanted to come and get a good look at the island,' was his response to Kirsty's query. 'So I said I would land them just and let them find their own way about. They'll not come to any harm,' he finished.

'How long would they be wanting to look around?'

He shrugged. 'The Dear only knows. They say they want to look for any kind of wild herbs and shrubs and things. I don't know what like of work the man does but I would think myself he is likely to be a doctor of some sort. The lassie, his daughter, is said to be studying for a degree of some sort at a college in Canada.'

'Oh my, but isn't she the bonny lassie right enough,' interposed Euan Ally. 'Bonny enough to make an ornament, is that not so Jamie?' He treated Kirsty to a conspiratorial wink. Jamie grunted, but dismissed the question.

'Wait now till you get a look at her,' Euan Ally advised with another heavy wink.

Kirsty was surprised. 'Am I likely to be getting a look at her,' she enquired. 'Did anyone say there would be a strupak for them if they wished for it?'

'Ach, they said Mhairi Jane had given them each a good poc of food and a flask of tea, so they'll likely not be wanting anything till they get back to Clachan.' Jamie spoke offhandedly, but she thought he seemed a little embarrassed, even a little flushed.

'They're staying with Mhairi Jane, did you say?'

'Aye, so they are. They'll not go hungry there.'

'That's true indeed,' agreed Kirsty, but all the same she would have liked to meet the subject of Euan Ally's winking, though undoubtedly Mhairi Jane would be more than keen to impart all the information she desired on the girl and her father when next they met. She shrugged off her slight feeling of disappointment and went on her way to where she expected to find the cows.

She was returning with her milk pail two-thirds full when she came across the couple, and when they paused to exchange greetings the lassie's eyes focused on the milk pail. It had never been a custom of Kirsty's to cover or even to carry a lid for the pail unless the rain was bucketing down so she was not too surprised when the lassie exclaimed, 'Daddy, just look at that milk! It's so creamy it's almost ochre coloured!' She looked at Kirsty. 'Is it Highland cows you have?'

Kirsty nodded. 'Highlanders just,' she acknowledged. 'They give little enough milk but what they give is butter almost before it gets into the churn.'

The lassie sighed.

'They seem to be going in more for shorthorn crosses in Clachan,' the man observed.

'I believe there's a better sale for them on the mainland than the Highlanders, though myself I wouldn't wish to change,' Kirsty told him.

'Oh, no indeed,' agreed the lassie. 'They're so picturesque,' she added. 'But are they not more savage than the cows with shorter horns?'

'They are not!' stated Kirsty emphatically. 'Even a Highland bull is kinder both to his cows and to his

89

herdsman than is a shorthorn. Our own bull here is as gentle as a calf.' She started to move away. 'If the young lady would wish for a taste from my pail I would be willing for her to do that as soon as I get back to the house and put it through the sieve.'

'Oh yes please Pop. Why don't we?' cried the lassie eagerly.

The man smiled indulgently. 'I think we should at least introduce ourselves to the kind lady first, don't you my dear.' He held out his hand to Kirsty. 'I'm Hugh Roberton from Montreal,' he said. His handclasp was reassuringly firm and friendly. 'And this is my daughter Claudine, though we call her Dina for short.' Kirsty smiled and offered her hand.

'And what brings you to these parts,' she inquired politely.

'Dina's studying for a degree in botany,' Hugh Roberton replied. 'And I believe my mother came from somewhere in the islands so we took the chance of a holiday here to look around.'

'We've met your son maybe?' he continued after a moment. 'The dark handsome young man who brought us across in his boat?'

'Folks say he is handsome,' Kirsty admitted, without disputing the relationship.

'And there was a young fellow called Ally. They say they will be taking us back to Clachan before it gets dark. They told us we are to go down to the shore when we are ready.'

'Then I will be going back to the house now,' Kirsty told them. 'You will be for coming along with me, or you will be for coming along later?' Her tone was interrogative, hoping they would choose the latter alternative which they did. She indicated the track they should follow. 'You will see the house just so soon as you reach the top of the rise, and you will be sure to find me thereabouts.'

'We're not likely to get lost?' the lassie enquired light-heartedly.

Kirsty bestowed on her a teasing smile. 'Only if you choose to be very foolish and walk into a cave instead of following along the track,' she responded with mock gravity.

'Dina is quite capable of doing that,' her father warned. 'If she thinks there might be something interesting inside.' They were all laughing as Kirsty prepared to resume her path.

'Is there only one house on the island?' Hugh Roberton asked.

'Only one that is more than a ruin,' Kirsty confirmed. 'You will not miss it.'

The couple conferred for a moment and then the man called, 'We aim to follow you in a while. We have to keep our eyes skinned to see if we find any herbs or shrubs that we haven't found elsewhere.'

'That will be fine,' responded Kirsty. 'Till I see you again then.' She gestured a farewell.

It was well into the evening before they arrived at the house. There was a kettle boiling and a pile of pancakes fresh from the girdle beside the hob. 'You will take a wee strupak?' Kirsty enquired, as she invited them to seat themselves on the bench while she poured two mugs of tea. She handed Dina a mug of milk.

'Gee whizz, but isn't this wonderful!' Hugh Roberton enthused as he bit into a pancake. 'Ma'am, this is a wonderful island; we've had a wonderful day, and now this wonderful hospitality. A grand day, wouldn't you say honey?'

'Mmm. Super,' Dina nodded vigorously; her mouth was full of pancake. 'I'd say this is downright cosy, wouldn't you Pop?' She sipped the milk as she might have tasted nectar.

Her father voiced his hearty agreement while smilingly indicating that she should wipe the milky moustache from her mouth. Kirsty, mistrusting the fervour of their compliments, pushed the dish of pancakes towards them with a gesture of invitation and as they continued chatting and enjoying their strupak she busied herself with unimportant tasks about the kitchen while covertly observing them. Dina, she reckoned would be about eighteen to twenty years old and certainly she was a good-looking girl. Not 'bonny' as Euan Ally had implied, but slender with dainty hands and merry brown eyes and an abundance of fair to tawny hair which, though confined by a blue clasp, looked as if it might be impatient to be released into a riot of bouncy curls. Her smile-shaped mouth, her white teeth and her creamy skin enlivened by a mere sprinkle of freckles all combined to make her into a very attractive young woman. But, Kirsty wondered, since Euan Ally had so recently married Enac who was herself, in island terms, 'a truly bonny lassie' why had he seemed so impressed? Had his praise and fierce winking been intended to convey to her that Jamie had displayed some interest in the girl? She suspected it might be so. Indeed, she found herself hoping it was so. Jamie's indifference to any girls in the vicinity had seemed to her natural enough in view of his sometimes fierce condemnation of their enforced piety and the shortcomings of his own religious upbringing, but she'd had no doubt of his eventually meeting some lassie who would appeal to him. She herself would not have envisaged Dina as a likely partner for him but, she reasoned, it would surely be good for him, even temporarily, to enjoy a taste of female company. She'd never allowed herself to think that he might become a shy, repressed old bachelor like his father and his uncle – a fate which seemed too often to overtake so many island men. Jamie was just too handsome; too agile; too full of the joys of life; too kindly and considerate to be passed over in such a way. He would one day make some lassie an enviable husband – of that she was quite certain.

'Would I have your permission to smoke my pipe?' Hugh Roberton's request interrupted her musings. She assented willingly, continuing to observe him while he lit it. He would, she judged, be about the same height as herself but leaner, though his shoulders were broad in contrast. Beneath his tan his face showed a light fuzz, leading her to surmise that he had not bothered to shave since he'd arrived in Clachan. She guessed he was in his early forties though his crisp grey hair could have been deceptive. She wondered if, way back in Montreal, there was a wife waiting patiently for his return; whether there were other children; whether or not he was a widower.

Jamie appeared in the doorway. 'I thought I might find you here,' he announced.

Hugh Roberton twisted in his seat. 'I hope we haven't kept you waiting,' he apologised. 'The truth is that we've been enjoying your mother's hospitality. Splendid pancakes and hot tea and creamy milk. We must have missed noticing it was getting towards dark.'

'It's not that just,' Jamie told him. 'But there's a mist coming in over the hills and there's a threat of a breeze blowing up. Not that it'll be anything worth noticing on the sea but it might make it pretty wet and slippery landing on the rocks at Clachan seeing the tide is going back.'

'So you want to start back right away?'

'It's for yourself to say,' Jamie insisted. 'I am ready to take you back when you are ready to go just.'

Wordlessly Dina listened to the exchange, her eyes fixed on Jamie.

'Well honey, what do you want to do? Do you want to chance the weather and risk getting wet feet or would you rather go back now?' asked her father.

Dina's eyes were still on Jamie as if awaiting his bidding. Satisfied with his barely perceptible nod of approval she said, 'I think we should go back now.'

They gathered up their rucksacks, said their thank yous and asked quite eagerly if they could come again whenever they might be in Clachan.

Kirsty accompanied them down to the shore. It seemed natural that she and Hugh Roberton should walk together while Jamie and Dina followed behind, but Kirsty was surprised to see no sign of Euan Ally waiting down at the cove.

'Ach no, he's needing to stay with his uncle to give a hand with a job that's to be done before the light goes,' Jamie explained, dumping the two rucksacks into the dinghy before settling the father and daughter in the stern.

There were cordial farewells as Jamie rowed out to *The Two Ruaris*. Kirsty stood at the edge of the water and watched as the anchor came aboard and the boat set off across the rippled Sound.

chapter ten

By the end of May, summer was being ushered in by gentle southerly winds that smoothed the sea, encouraging it to reflect the blue skies. It brought an abundance of larks to fill the air with their exuberant outpourings of song, and while corncrakes rasped in the evenings, cuckoos seemed to be calling and gurgling from dawn to dusk. The scent of bluebells wafted across the island to mingle with the lingering smells of bog myrtle and bell-heather; the varying pinks of lousewort began to share the moorland with yellow tormentils, while hassocks of sturdy thrift bedizened the rocks and boulders that skirted the shore. On the Sound guillemots bobbed and divers, both red-throated and great northern, returned to prospect for fish and to call and renew their trysts with their chosen mates; rafts of eider duck exclaimed and gossiped their way around the bay, sounding for all the world like parties of scandal-mongering spinsters.

Euan Ally's Uncle Lachy had started work on what he persisted in calling 'Ally's Castle' and was getting on well; 'the boys' had overhauled *The Two Ruaris* after her winter lay-up and had started on the season's fishing, reporting good catches but grumbling that, as a consequence, prices were disappointingly low. All the same, it was plain to see their satisfaction that they were once again in contention with the sea.

On the croft the potatoes were growing staunchly, their green tops unaffected by the occasional tousling of the wind; the grass looked promising and the corn was growing satisfactorily. The peats, cut earlier in the spring, were now drying on the peat island prior to being ferried over and stacked against the house for winter use. The cattle were flourishing, their shaggy coats combed and sleeked by the wind, and Euan Ally's small flock of sheep were eagerly familiarising themselves with the Westisle grazing. Soon Enac was able to boast that their 'Castle' now had firm set walls and a roof which was in the process of being securely wedged and weighted, roped and tied ready to defy the assault of the severest winter gale. It also boasted a chimney stack, topped by a chimney pot that would not have looked out of place on a mansion.

'My, it's going to be a house fit for a rich man just,' Enac declared delightedly.

'And for the coming bairn,' added Euan Ally.

Momentarily surprised, Kirsty looked at Enac.

'Aye, I reckon I'm carrying a bairn,' confirmed Enac. 'It'll be due about Hogmanay maybe.'

Kirsty held both of Enac's arms for a moment in silent congratulation.

That same evening Willy John brought over a boatload of Clachan folk, catching Kirsty unawares. Although she was feeling tired after a long day's work weeding and earthing the potatoes, the sound of happy voices and the exchange of warm greetings, followed by the appreciative comments on the strupak she hastily provided, dispelled any tiredness. Kirsty was soon enjoying the ensuing ceilidh.

As the gentleness of the season continued, the evening cruises became more frequent. It was as if Clachan had newly discovered Westisle as a venue where they could count on a welcome and be sure of enjoying themselves. Kirsty assumed it was more likely the presence of Enac and Euan Ally that brought over most of the younger folks while the older people were no doubt curious to see what sort of job Lachy was making of the rebuilding of 'Ally's Castle'; whatever brought them, there was no doubt the cruise parties were highly popular and enjoyed by young and old.

'As good as a concert,' Enac was heard to announce one evening when the postman had brought his melodeon; the bus driver had brought his bagpipes and the dancing, skirling, wisecracking and whooping had become wild enough to attract the attention of homing gulls which hovered low, interrupting shrilly and raucously as if competing with or remonstrating against the hilarity.

Another evening Kirsty herself heard one ancient pipe smoker observe to his equally ancient crony, 'I'm saying a ceilidh like this is near as good as New Year.'

'More better,' had come the considered reply. 'I'm after thinking a ceilidh like this is as good as a dose of salts. It kind of loosens the cac in you so that it's no effort to go out on the moors the next day.'

'An' there's no missionary on the island that can condemn us.'

'Aye indeed. No missionary in sight nor sound nor hearing that can give an account of it,' agreed his companion discreetly. Two heads nodded in tacit understanding as pipes were replaced and puffed at complacently. Kirsty reminded herself that the two old men belonged to the generation that feared the con-demnation of the missionary rather more than the wrath of the Almighty.

Occasionally, one or two 'touries' might be permitted to join an evening cruise, so long as they were agile enough to clamber aboard a small and often leaky boat without protesting that their feet were getting wet. They had also to accept that the trip had no scheduled departure or return time. A tentative enquiry as to a departure time might have elicited a phlegmatic, 'Ach, it'll not be till Fergus or Willy or whoever is back from taking his cow to the bull,' or some such excuse. A timid entreaty as to when they could expect to see their beds that night might bring the insouciant response, 'Not until the sun has hidden itself at the back of yon black sgurr and is thinking of showing itself out the other side I reckon.' With such hazy information the enquirer would have to be content, so it was only the adventurous or totally indifferent souls who would risk the trip.

There was indeed never any urgency about the return trip to Clachan unless the bus driver had chosen to be a member of the party when naturally there was a loosely approximate time imposed so that the bus could leave Clachan near enough its scheduled departure. Otherwise, since during the spring and summer there was only a perfunctory dimming of the light and no real darkness, the Clachanites' disregard of clock time was patent and the ceilidhing would continue well into the early hours of the morning. Not even the most senile members of the party ever admitted tiredness. Work might tire them but revelry appeared to be a stimulus.

They had no need to worry about the cattle since they would be out on the hill with calves at foot, so there would be no distended udders needing to be relieved; the poultry would very likely have been sent for their 'summer holiday', that is, they would have been banished to the moors where they would virtually fend for themselves until the autumn with no more than a roughly built sod shelter to serve as a retreat from any really wild or wet weather or to provide privacy for egg-laying. Any eggs not filched by predatory rats, stoats, or hoody crows would be collected by the children after their release from school.

When Westisle hosted an evening cruise there was little enough rest for Kirsty, but she was content to mentally store the sounds of laughter and merrymaking to recall during the bleak short days of winter and the long nights when there was likely to be no sound save the roar of the sea and the steady throbbing of wind against the house.

It was shortly after the commencement of the English school summer holidays that a letter arrived from the English couple telling Kirsty that they expected to be in Clachan the following week and asking if they could be collected whenever possible. The first suitable day happened to be the first day of Wee Ruari's school summer holidays and since it was a Friday Jamie took the fishing boat across to Clachan to collect all three of them.

Kirsty did not go down to watch for the boat's return but waited at the door. She was not expecting her son to come rushing into the house as he normally did, being sure he would regard it as his duty, even his right, to escort the young couple to the house.

'They're here!' She heard his shout at the same time as she spied them coming along the track, the couple carrying their camping gear, Wee Ruari laden with his end-of-term exercise books.

'Jamie let me bring the boat some of the way by myself,' he announced, with breathless excitement.

'My, my,' Kirsty complimented him. 'You'll soon be taking yourself to school and bringing yourself back home again the way you're coming on.' She greeted the young couple warmly. 'It is a fine day for crossing,' she said. 'You will be taking a wee strupak before you unpack?'

'No, no,' refused the young man hurriedly. 'We'd like to get the tent up pretty quickly, maybe fairly close to your house temporarily if you don't mind, and then we would be very grateful if we could come and enjoy one of your strupaks.'

'Yes, we've great memories of your strupaks,' the young woman's voice sounded almost nostalgic.

'Do as you please just,' Kirsty indicated a site near the barn. 'Your tent would be safe enough there I reckon, away from the cattle, and any hens you can shoo out of the way just.'

Hardly had she settled back to her chores when there was another interruption. Willy Joe arrived with a passenger in his boat and Kirsty found herself shaking hands with a squat dark man whose eyebrows resembled shaggy tweed.

'Dugan's been gamekeeper since he was hardly more than a wee laddie, for some Lord or other that's died over-by in Appin, is that not so Dugan?' Willy Joe introduced his passenger.

Dugan nodded modest confirmation.

'An' he's over in Clachan seein' his sister that was married to Tearlach Mor's brother till he passed on, and now he'd like fine to see how Westisle's doin' since both Ruaris have passed on,' Willy Joe finished his introduction.

'Aye indeed,' admitted Dugan, 'and I'm after hearing Euan Ally has got himself wed and has got his Uncle Lachy to sort one of the old but and bens for himself and his wife to live in.' His tone was a mixture of surprise and censure.

'He seemed keen enough to have it that way,' Kirsty acknowledged.

'And they're telling me he's getting a fair-sized croft to go with it?'

'We agreed a fair amount of land.'

'And he will be bringing over his sheep?'

'I believe that to be his intention.' Kirsty forbore from disclosing to Dugan that Euan Ally's sheep were already enjoying Westisle grazing.

'Aye well, right enough, but I reckon you and 'the boys' will be needing to have a good muirburn next Spring,' he commented after a few moments' meditation.

She thought he had a homespun kind of voice that urged her to trust him.

'I'd be glad of any advice you could give me,' she invited, offering him the obligatory strupach.

'Well then, you mightn't be doing so bad for yourself to rent out a bit of grouse-shooting when the time comes,' he suggested. 'I believe the two Ruaris wouldn't hear of such a thing though they could have done well enough out of it.

You have a deal too many grouse on the island to my way of thinking.'

'Indeed, do I not know it just,' Kirsty exclaimed. 'Haven't I said plenty of times to the Clachan men that they're welcome to come and do a bit of shooting but though they're well enough pleased to come and shoot rabbits they scoff at wasting cartridges on the grouse. Myself I would like fine to hear less of the birds shouting "Go back, go back" every time I'm out on the moors. But Clachan folk won't eat grouse so they won't shoot them.'

'They won't eat them,' echoed Dugan derisively. 'Ach, Clachan folk always was daft anyway. Mind you, I reckon it's the women's way of cooking the birds likely. They don't boil so well in a pot so my wife tells me. I never ate them myself till I got a wife that baked them in the oven.' He gestured towards the range. 'You have an oven there, if it gets hot at all.'

'It gets hot enough,' Kirsty told him. 'It cooks grand pies and cakes and things so long as it has plenty of peats. Maybe if Jamie would bring me a couple of grouse I could cook them along with some potatoes, but I doubt neither of "the boys" would have an appetite for such, though I myself would like fine to try them.'

'Aye, then that must be the way of it,' concluded Dugan. Thanking her for the strupak he rose to go. 'I'd best be away to take a look at how Lachy is getting on with the building of "Ally's Castle",' he joked. 'And then Willy Joe will be for taking me back to Clachan.'

As they shook hands he said, 'If you get to feeling you might want to let a bit of shooting, get word to me just, and I'll see what I can do.' He paused for a moment and then added, 'Maybe you could put up one or two folk that would come for the shooting?'

Kirsty smiled. 'Maybe I could do that just,' she agreed without enthusiasm.

'You could keep it at the back of your mind maybe,' he insisted.

'Just so,' she agreed, but she knew that at the back of her mind it must stay for a long time.

Dugan nodded approval and, with a final farewell, set off with Willy Joe over the hill. No sooner had they left than the English couple came into the kitchen, preceded by Wee Ruari.

'We think we've got the tent firmly pitched,' they said. 'So we'll accept that cup of tea if it's still on offer.'

'Tea is always on offer in this kitchen,' chirped Wee Ruari. 'See, there's steam coming out of that kettle and that one.'

Kirsty tried to silence him with a gesture, but realising he was likely to monopolise the conversation until his mouth was full of food she allowed him to continue. Somewhat to her surprise, the young couple seemed eager to talk about and anxious to again visit the old settlement. As it was still early evening they wanted to decide, with Lachy's approval, which of the old habitations they would choose to have rebuilt for their proposed summer dwelling.

During the winter, Kirsty had grown sceptical of their desire to have a permanent summer residence on Westisle, telling herself that their early enthusiasm would doubtless have waned by the time they had seriously balanced the facilities of city life against the frustrations and rigours of life on Westisle. Listening to them again, after they had returned from visiting the old settlement and were once again comfortably ensconced in her kitchen, there appeared to be little doubt as to the seriousness of their intention.

'For so long as it lasts,' murmured Jamie cynically, when she later remarked to him on their apparent enthusiasm.

'I believe they're keen enough yet,' Enac supplied. 'I was over with them now just, when they were speaking to Lachy about their ideas and trying to get him to say when he reckons he can start work.'

'They've spoken to him already! And what did Lachy have to say to them?' Kirsty still tended to be dubious of Lachy's willingness to take on such work for total strangers. She was anxious to hear what his reactions had been when the couple had pressed him about their plans.

'Ach, he told them it would likely be next summer before he would be fit to start even thinking on it and when they said that seemed to be a long time to wait he told them if they still had a mind that way they could hasten it by hauling good strong driftwood from the shore and putting it where it would be handy enough for him. Not that just but he showed them the right kind of building stones and told them to pile them near at hand.'

Kirsty expressed her astonishment.

'Ach, he still mocked them to Euan Ally and me saying they'd never wish to spend a whole summer in a wild place like Westisle, but they've either convinced him they're serious enough just or he's after thinking it'll make a good story to tell at the winter ceilidhs.'

'And you think he's believing them enough to start working for them?' Kirsty queried.

'I reckon so right enough, if he's spared,' Enac said with a sardonic chuckle.

'I reckon so. If they leave him a good enough deposit,' quipped Euan Ally.

On the way back from milking the next day Kirsty took the path which would lead her near the old settlement and its dilapidated cottages. She was struck by the way work on Euan Ally's chosen dwelling was progressing.

'My, my but I'm seeing a great difference already,' she complimented him and his uncle.

'Aye, it's coming along well enough,' they admitted brusquely as if resenting her appearance.

Kirsty always felt a little embarrassed in Uncle Lachy's presence as evidently he did in hers. Since he had landed on Westisle she had seen very little of him. Euan Ally's inexpert introduction had merely indicated to her that he was 'Lachy there' and after a nod and a brief handshake the man had ignored her. He'd either been instructed or had himself chosen to sleep in a bunk aboard *The Two Ruaris* and, according to 'the boys' he had brought with him a pot for his potatoes and fish which he cooked over a rough fireplace he'd built in a sheltered spot among the ruins. With the help of 'the boys' Kirsty ensured he was well supplied with oatcakes and scones but apart from that he wanted nothing from her, spurning all offers to share a meal with them in the house. Only twice so far had he been persuaded to come near enough to take a 'fly cup' and even then he'd insisted on it being taken outside for him to drink.

'You'd think he was safe enough here in the kitchen with you and the two boys to keep me from seducing him, wouldn't you,' she demanded of Enac one day when his bashfulness had seemed particularly irksome.

'Ach, when a man's a poacher and a precentor and has an old wifie that girns at him for so much as smiling on the Sabbath you canna expect him to be like other men. All the same,' she'd added after a pause, 'there's plenty say he's a fair comic when he's away with the men and has taken a good dram.'

Kirsty smiled. 'I can believe that well enough,' she allowed.

'And he's said to be the best man in these parts and beyond when it comes to a bit of building,' Enac championed.

'He seems to be a right lad o' pairts,' Kirsty commented.

'Aye, that's right enough,' Euan Ally confirmed as he came into the kitchen. 'He's after saying he'll get the roof finished if the weather holds.'

'And if he's spared don't forget,' Enac put in with assumed piety.

'He's saying to make sure the range comes the next time the boat's over so he'll be knowing what sort of space he has to make for it. You'd best write a letter telling them to make sure and send a chimney with it,' he reminded Enac.

She had spent most of the day gathering crotal from the rocks and was now massaging some of the cream which Kirsty had put aside for making butter into her knuckles.

'I'll see and write it tomorrow, for you to post next time you're in Clachan, ' she promised. 'My fingers is a bit sore tonight.'

'I'll be going across to Clachan first thing in the morning,' Euan Ally warned her, causing Enac to grimace. 'Lachy's needin' me to get a pair of his breeks from his wife seeing he sat in the sea yesterday and he's not got them anywhere near dry yet. I think he's feeling kind of uncomfortable at night since he doesn't take them off to sleep.'

Enac chortled. Kirsty was too prudent to offer to dry the wet trousers by hanging them over the kitchen range.

'How did he come to be sitting in the sea,' she enquired.

'Didn't he slip getting off the boat just. He was there no more than a minute or two or he might have drowned more than his breeks!'

Once the range had arrived and been installed at the 'Castle' and the chimney thoroughly tested and approved, Euan Ally and Enac lost no time in settling themselves into their new home. Uncle Lachy had begun, in response to ever more urgent pleas from Enac, to set about erecting a sturdy lean-to bothy at the back of the house large enough to accommodate her loom. She had already gathered enough crotal for the dying of the wool from the first shearing of their sheep flock and was anxious to begin weaving before the rest of the vegetable dyes succumbed to the winter. The English couple, hearing of her intention and becoming intrigued with the likelihood of there being a Westisle tweed, had extracted from her a pledge that she would allow them to purchase the first length she wove, pledging an adequate sum of money to ensure she remembered her promise. Enac was very pleased. She had been well tutored and had learned to weave good tweed even before her mother had died. She was more than eager to start work.

'So you had Dugan to see you,' Jamie questioned when he came in that night. 'He was wanting to see how we were getting on with Euan Ally's "Castle" since he's heard so much about it in Clachan.'

'He wanted to see how the island was doing now that the two Ruaris have passed on,' she apprised him, and went on, 'He says we could do with a good muirburn and also that we have too many grouse by far.'

'Aye, I believe he might be right enough about that,' agreed Jamie.

'He reckoned I could make a bit of money letting the shooting and even catering for a couple of guns: bed and a bowl of porridge only,' she stressed. 'He said to let him know if I had a mind for he could maybe send over one or two folk.'

'You're thinking on it?' Jamie queried.

'No, no,' she rejoined, 'but I said I would keep it at the back of my mind just.'

Jamie was quiet for a moment.

'It might be a good idea though,' he said. 'I reckon you could make two good bedrooms up in the loft, and you could maybe get Lachy started on it while he's still here,' he suggested.

This, she thought, coming from Jamie, sounded strangely out of character.

'That's a job that must wait until the cold weather is here, and you and Euan Ally are not so tied to the fishing,' she stated.

'Maybe so,' he agreed with a shrug.

He returned to the subject, however, one evening a few weeks later. Kirsty was ironing and Wee Ruari, who was home for the annual potato lifting, was preoccupied in fashioning some sort of animal shapes from corn stalks. A little exasperated at the urgency she imagined to be in Jamie's tone, she replied testily.

'Jamie, you're in that much haste to clear the loft I'm thinking you must know of some tourie that would be wishing to take a room here. Is that the way of it?' she probed.

'Ach, no one at all,' he responded quickly. 'And not until the summer comes anyway. But there's plenty of rubbish up there, and it's going to take a wee whiley to shift is it not?'

'It will surely,' she had to agree with him.

Wee Ruari held up his bunch of corn stalks and inspected it critically.

'I reckon that "some tourie" is that lassie you took a great liking to when she and her father were staying with Mhairi Jane in the summer,' he interjected innocently.

Kirsty looked at him in surprise.

Jamie shot the boy a repressive glance. 'There was no such lassie,' he denied hurriedly.

Unperturbed, Wee Ruari continued inspecting his corn stalks. 'Willie Bhan was after saying there was,' he insisted.

Jamie scowled. 'Then Willie Bhan was talking nonsense just,' he asserted and, snatching up a piece of rope that had been hanging over a chair, made for the door with what struck Kirsty as unseemly haste.

With eyebrows still raised she looked after him. Jamie had obviously been embarrassed but she forbore from asking Wee Ruari to reveal any other comments Willie Bhan might have made. Thoughtful, she continued ironing, letting her mind play around with the possibilities. If the Clachanites had suspected any hint of a romance between Jamie and the lassie who had briefly visited Westisle, he would indeed have suffered plenty of teasing, though none had reached her ears. She had noticed a kind of attraction between the pair but had assumed that the lassie's departure from Clachan had meant the end of the matter. Jamie had made no subsequent reference to the lassie, nor had he appeared to be in any way suffering from a sense of deprival. Could they have kept in touch? she asked herself. It seemed unlikely but she reminded herself that it was Jamie who collected all the mail and brought it to the island, and it was customary for him and Euan Ally to extract their own correspondence before handing the bag over to her. She would be ignorant of any contact between the couple unless Jamie himself had chosen to tell her. Was Wee Ruari right she wondered on reflection.

She finished the ironing, draped the fresh clothes over the rack, folded the ironing cloth and put it away in the cupboard. She was still pondering as she began to prepare the evening meal, gently chiding herself that perhaps she had been a trifle insensitive in dismissing the thought of there having been any lingering relationship between the lassie and Jamie. Perhaps she too should have indulged in a little light-hearted teasing. He could possibly have wanted to confide in her.

With a slight surge of misgiving she decided to start clearing out the loft, resolving to do it discreetly, not saying anything to Jamie but waiting for him to perhaps notice what was being done so that he could comment nonchalantly without suspecting she might have guessed the possible reason for any urgency. There was no urgency of course, for no touries would be prepared to come at this time of year. The plan worked. Shortly after she started not only Jamie but also Euan Ally and Enac made time to help dispose of the piles of old netting, sacks of ropes and other miscellaneous fishing gear which was of no further use.

111

Kirsty was dragging a bundle to the head of the stairs when she heard Enac exclaim excitedly. Kirsty joined her in the corner of the room.

'Is it not beautiful just!' Enac had shifted a pile of netting and was gazing at something which had been hidden below it.

Kirsty caught her breath as she saw Wee Ruari's' old cradle, her mind jumping instantly to the memory of the man who had lovingly carved it; the man who had given her his heart but who, out of respect for his brother, had never let her know until he lay on his deathbed. For a moment she was unable to speak.

'Ruari Mor carved it himself when Wee Ruari was born,' she managed to say after a few moments. 'He was good with his hands.'

'Indeed, he must have been,' enthused Enac, running her hands over the polished wood.

Kirsty suddenly knew what she had to say.

'You must have it for your bairn mo ghaoil,' she offered. 'It is surely of no further use in this house.'

Enac demurred politely, but couldn't restrain her pleasure when finally prevailed upon to accept. She went searching for Euan Ally to tell him while Kirsty, glad to be alone for a moment, let her thoughts drift back to that halcyon period when, her baby gurgling in her arms, she was probably more content than at any other time in her life. The sound of footsteps on the stairs brought her back to the present; with a slight feeling of weariness she went back to her tidying.

It was Enac who, it seemed apropos of nothing, put the question that Kirsty would have liked to ask Jamie.

'When was Mhairi Jane after saying that yon professor and his daughter had booked to come and stay with her?'

'I believe it will be sometime in the summer,' said Jamie with a show of indifference.

'I reckon they might be wanting to stay a few days over here then,' Kirsty observed. 'They seemed to find plenty to interest them.'

She caught Euan Ally's covert glance at Jamie as if expecting some reaction, but none was forthcoming.

When the loft was finally cleared they decided that it was indeed big enough for two reasonable bedrooms, despite the slope of the roof reducing headroom at the sides. Timber was brought from the mainland and Lachy, Enac's lean-to being finished, was prevailed upon to risk his eternal soul and come into the widow's house to erect the partitions and door frames. He had only completed the basics however when, saying he felt the breath of autumn on the wind, he returned to Clachan in good time for the serious deer-poaching season. He had undertaken to return 'with the spring and the spiders' if the English couple were still of a mind for him to build up their chosen ruin into a holiday cottage. He had added to that, 'if the Lord spares me', a proviso which Enac dismissed with a contemptuous, 'More like if his wife will allow him out of her sight for that length of time again.'

After Jamie and Euan Ally had, a little inexpertly, put the finishing touches to the woodwork, Kirsty and Enac set to with paint brushes while 'the boys' brought wax-cloth for the floor, two beds, two chests of drawers and two cupboards from the mainland. They also obtained two cured sheepskins from the Clachan shepherd which Kirsty brushed and combed to make two soft mats to lay beside the beds.

'I reckon these are rooms fit for lords and ladies,' gloated Enac.

'Aye, I'd say they were good enough,' agreed Euan Ally. 'What do you think Jamie?'

'Right,' murmured Jamie, looking a trifle impatient at being asked his opinion on a matter which he wished to be regarded as unworthy of his attention.

Kirsty surveyed the room critically.

'It's me that's the loon for forgetting to ask you to get me four jugs and two basins from the stores when you were on the mainland. Maybe you'll get them the next time you go.'

Jamie looked at her enquiringly.

'They'll need to have somewhere to wash themselves,' she explained.

'But why four jugs and only two basins,' he asked.

'They'll need hot water as well as cold surely,' Kirsty reminded him. 'Touries won't be content to splash their faces with a handful of cold water the same as you and Euan Ally just.'

'Aye, I suppose,' he sounded unconvinced.

'And any gentleman that would wish to come might wish to shave himself,' Enac was quick to point out. 'You would need to give them hot water on Saturdays anyway, so they could shave ready for the Sabbath.'

Recalling her time at the boarding house, Islay, Kirsty observed knowledgeably, 'It's natural enough for some men to wish to shave every day, not only for the Sabbath just.'

'Then I reckon they must be mighty proud of themselves,' commented Jamie dryly.

'On the mainland I believe there's plenty that does Jamie,' Euan Ally assured him. 'And if they don't they leave their beards be until there's enough growth to cut with scissors.'

'Or sheep shears,' chuckled Enac.

chapter eleven

The Sound swiftly began to take on its wintry aspect; the hill peaks beyond Clachan rarely shed their thick pelts of dark cloud, against which background the occasional speculative gull appeared to have been bleached white. *The Two Ruaris* had been laid up in her winter berth, leaving only the small and less seaworthy *Katy* to make any necessary trips to Clachan to take or bring Wee Ruari to or from school. When Brachty, the only cow that was being milked, decided for herself that she wished to have the shelter of the byre at night and began to present herself at the gate of the croft as soon as she perceived the dusk beginning to deepen, Kirsty knew it was the portent of more turbulent weather. It started with a roaring gale that was almost dizzying in its savagery and which continued with no noticeable moderation for close on three weeks. It confined her son to Clachan and with each successive day Kirsty grew more and more despondent but, despite her earnest prayers and entreaties to the Almighty, the wind showed no sign of slackening sufficiently to enable the *Katy* to cross the Sound to collect Wee Ruari. She grew daily more tense as the school winter holidays approached. And Christmas day was coming! Christmas had never been celebrated nor even alluded to during her own childhood and youth but when she had worked in the boarding house she had learned from the conversation of English visitors of what an exciting day it was in England; of how the children looked forward, often for many weeks, to the visit of some Father Christmas who would bring them presents; of how he would expect the house to be decorated to welcome him; of how he would bring them invitations to lots of parties. It had all sounded so intriguing that as soon as her son had reached the age of two she had introduced him to the idea of there being some small but very special recognition of Christmas Day. She'd even marked it with red crayon each year on the agricultural calendar so she herself would not forget. Presents such as shop toys were out of the question, of course, since north of Glasgow few places recognised Christmas and only then in a desultory fashion. Parties were impossible with but one child on the island and precious little likelihood of there being any winter transport even if other children would be permitted or indeed would want to come. So far each year, she'd managed to bake a special sort of cake and decorate it as best she could. Jamie's last visit to the mainland had surprisingly yielded a box of sweeties which had joined the cake already in the oatmeal bin keeping fresh. The sweeties were called coconut kisses and they were pink and white and sugary so she was sure Wee Ruari would love them. She'd baked shortbread in easily identifiable shapes of men and animals and fish, which she would wrap in a piece of bleached flour sack tied with coloured tape or twine saved from parcels sent by the English couple, to give as a Christmas present along with the new jersey she'd been knitting for him. She always

117

knitted a jersey for him at Christmas-time and he always appeared overjoyed to get it. She'd spied out a few small twigs of greenery, but had left them outside ready to bring in on Christmas morning to decorate the house. But still the gales raged on, making the crossing to Clachan unthinkable.

Kirsty knew she could not console herself, as she had at Halloween, that her son would have more fun in Clachan with his school friends since, so far as the children were concerned, once Halloween was over their year's merry-making ceased. The school would be closed for the scheduled end-of-year holiday but it was generally assumed that the closure was primarily to give the teachers a break so as to prepare themselves for the important celebration of Hogmanay. To the children it meant little more than being available for extra chores like carrying peats or water from the well or hay to the cattle out-wintering on the moors. And yet there were no sulks! Such work was part of growing up which was exciting enough. Such fun as they had was mainly derived from watching the normally dour and strait-laced adults growing daily more absurd as they steadily imbibed the spirit(s) of the New Year!

It was not until four days after the official school holiday had begun that Kirsty woke from an uneasy sleep to the sudden realisation that the wind had ceased to thud against the walls and roof of the house. Reckoning the calendar would be declaring it to be the day before Christmas Day, she rose swiftly and dressed, intending to hurry along to Jamie's room and waken him to the knowledge of the calm but as soon as she opened her bedroom door she saw there was already lamplight in the kitchen and Jamie was bending over the stove stirring a pan of brose.

Her heart leaped. 'Oh Jamie, are you thinking maybe the weather has settled enough for you to get across to Clachan?' Her voice was taut with muted hopefulness but, born and bred in the islands as she had been, she knew only too well that no woman must ever urge a seaman to risk combat with an angry sea against his better judgement. She waited tensely to hear his verdict.

'I reckon it might be, but there'll still be a good swell in it,' he replied.

Kirsty breathed a little easier. His tone had inspired confidence and she allowed herself to think about the possibility of the celebration going ahead as planned. Even though it was still too dark to assess the conditions in the Sound she felt she could safely begin her final preparations.

It was barely light when Euan Ally arrived.

'There's a good roar of swell out there yet,' he said to Jamie.

'Aye, I reckon there will be,' Jamie agreed.

But as the day lightened the sea calmed, though the crash of the swell along the shore could still be heard. Euan Ally and Jamie had gone outside for a look at the weather but were soon back to announce that they would be away to Clachan within the hour. Kirsty murmured a grateful thanks to the Almighty and spurred herself to briskness, happily humming a tune as new ideas for pleasing Wee Ruari darted into her head.

The day was darkening again when her son came bounding into the kitchen.

'I'm here,' he announced himself, quickly discarding his oilskin and sou'wester and kicking off his gumboots.

'I see you're here,' she responded warmly, pressing her hands on his shoulders. 'Aye, and you've grown a few more inches I believe since I last saw you.' She would have liked to hug him but knew he would dodge away.

He backed against the door frame where Jamie had always marked in pencil his height at each holiday from school.

'You've topped the last one at potato lifting I believe,' Kirsty exclaimed, squinting at the wall. 'Jamie will tell you for sure as soon as he's back.' She buttered a scone and gave it to him.

He stuffed a good half of it into his mouth before speaking thickly, 'Ally's Uncle Lachy has given him a haunch of venison for Hogmanay.'

'Indeed! So they won't go short over the holiday as Enac had begun to fear, with the weather being as bad as it has been.'

'Ach, Ally could always kill one of his sheep,' Wee Ruari said offhandedly. 'Will I get my jersey now? It *is* what you say is Christmas, isn't it?'

'It is indeed, tomorrow,' she confirmed, pleased that he had remembered. 'And you'll get your jersey fresh to put on in the morning. You'd best take a wash tonight seeing there's a good fire.'

'Will it need to be a tub wash?' he asked sheepishly.

'Seeing it's Christmas,' she soothed. 'I think you need it.'

'I'll not be needing to take another for Hogmanay?' he demanded combatively.

'No, no, I reckon this one will do for you until the sea gets warm enough for you to go into it.'

Grumpily, he dragged the half wooden tub from out the back, set it in front of the fire and sat watching disapprovingly as she tipped hot and then cold water into it. His complaint against taking tub washes, even once a year was, he said, because it made him feel different from all the other children he knew. Clachan scholars would have been scornful if they'd heard he had to submit to an annual tub wash; he himself suspected she was trying to make him too English in his habits. However, when she indicated that the water was at the right temperature, he got into the tub quickly and, crouching down, commanded her to stand by with a towel so that he could nip out instantly at the first sound of Jamie coming. His ablutions were done swiftly and splashily but thoroughly and he was already into his warmed nightshirt before Jamie came into the kitchen.

'It looks as if it's been a wet night,' Jamie observed, glancing at the floor.

'I've had my tub wash,' Wee Ruari told him. 'Now will you measure me against the door frame to see how much I've grown?'

'I doubt you will have grown since you were last here for the potato lifting. More likely you will have been smallened by the muck that's washed off you. But surely I'll mark your height if that's what you want.'

'Mam says she thinks I've grown,' insisted Wee Ruari.

Jamie studied the measurements on the doorframe. 'My! I believe she's right,' he asserted. 'Are you sure the Widow Fraser isn't after putting manure in your boots every morning to make you grow?'

Wee Ruari shook his head in solemn denial. 'No, it's not manure she uses, it's the stuff she gathers on the moors to

121

wash my stockings. She reckons it makes everything grow. Even her hens lay bigger eggs than anyone else's.'

'Aye well, we'll take her word for that,' Jamie allowed.

Kirsty slid hot potato scones off the girdle onto a wooden slab, along with a chunk of butter and a bowl of crowdie. She brewed a pot of tea and, after an enquiring glance at Jamie, filled his mug. She filled another one for herself and a mug of milk for her son. Neither of them seemed to be in their usual hurry to eat.

'Nobody interested in food?' she asked.

'Not so,' said Jamie at the end of a long yawn. He got up, stretched himself and then sat down again. 'I'll take a scone just, and then I'll maybe go and lay me down for a wee whiley,' and continued, 'Euan Ally's Uncle Lachy would have us go up to his house for a Hogmanay dram and then his aunty put out a kind of crusty bun and told us we must eat it and then we had to have another dram to wash it down and then the shepherd arrived with his bottle. Ach! you know the way things take on just,' he explained. 'I reckon I was ready for a lie down well before we left Clachan.'

Kirsty smiled understandingly. 'I'm thinking I'll maybe take this cup of tea just and then I'll be making for my own bed. I'll have a world of work to do tomorrow.' She glanced enquiringly at her son.

'What about bed now?' she urged, and as he raised his head in dazed enquiry, pursued. 'Are you no hearing Jamie saying he's away to his bed?'

There came a grunted reply. Since Euan Ally and Enac had settled in their 'Castle', Wee Ruari had proudly announced he was going to sleep in Jamie's bedroom; he seemed to think it made him more grown up. He stood up and stretched as Jamie had done, mumbled a sleepy 'Oidhche mhath' and lumbered off in Jamie's wake.

Kirsty was left alone to finish wrapping her son's presents ready for the morning. Satisfied, she finished her tea, turned down the lamp and took it into her own bedroom.

Before the dawn the snow had come, falling meekly it seemed, as if offering contrition for the savage spell of weather that had preceded it. Kirsty awoke to a white and silent world. She could see a few identifiable rabbit imprints near the house but the snow near the hen-house appeared undisturbed and she guessed the hens, or maybe only the cockerel which always led them out, had been reluctant to leave the shelter of the shed. Instead of the morning assembly of speculative hoodies there were only one or two birds stationed on the tops of the hay and corn stacks overlooking the feeding area and ready to swoop the moment they espied the possibility of food. Shivering, she encouraged the still hot ash in the kitchen grate to flames and with the aid of bellows and a pail of dry peats soon had two big kettles beginning to steam promisingly.

Pulling on thick stockings and gumboots she then tied an ancient overcoat over her thick homespun skirt with a length of rope, crammed on her ancient black beret, shrunken now after many drenchings, and pulled it down well over her ears. Knowing there was a spade handy within reach of the door, she set out to clear the snow so as to be able to feed the hens. It seemed that it was only a moment later that she heard a shout and turned to see Wee Ruari, barefooted and wearing only an old jacket over his nightshirt, shuffling hastily after her and exclaiming delightedly as he gathered handfuls of snow to throw at her. Lightly reproving him for his bare feet she aimed handfuls back in his direction. He responded eagerly, his cheeks glowing fiery red, his laughter seeming to invigorate the morning.

'I'm going to make a big, big snowball and throw it at Jamie to wake him from his bed,' he gloated excitedly.

'You'd best get well out of his way first,' she cautioned as he ran back to the house.

She'd finished feeding the hens before Jamie came out propelling a protesting Wee Ruari by the scruff of his neck and the seat of his pants. She noted with satisfaction that her son now wore boots and stockings.

'Jamie's going to make me a slidey,' he cried exultantly as he was hustled towards the barn where there was always a stack of driftwood and old fish boxes.

'You'll both need to come and take your porridge first,' she stipulated. She was not expecting them to comply but they were back and eager for breakfast within a surprisingly short time.

'My slidey is ready,' Wee Ruari announced between eager gulps of porridge. 'Jamie says it can be a Christmas present from him like I get from you. Will I get my new jersey now and will I bring in my new slidey to show you?'

'No, you will not bring your slidey indoors,' Jamie interrupted firmly. 'Slideys are not for indoors.'

'I'll come outside and take a look at it directly,' Kirsty was quick to console. 'And you'll get your new jersey as soon as you're back from telling Euan Ally and Enac that they're to be sure to come ceilidhing this evening and share our Christmas feast. That is the time you will be getting your presents.'

She looked at Jamie. 'I will be best pleased if he will be going along with you,' she said.

Jamie nodded. 'He can be coming along with me to the cows first,' he agreed.

'I can take my slidey,' offered Wee Ruari immediately. 'They'll maybe wish to ride back on it like those people on the card you got from the English couple.'

'No, you will not take your slidey,' said Jamie, stifling the expected protest by saying, 'Even if they would like a ride, it would not stand their weight and you yourself would not be strong enough to drag it over the moorland. It is best left here till we get back.' He pulled an oilskin over his jacket.

'Come on now. Let's be away,' he commanded hurriedly. 'I'm thinking there's more snow to come shortly and the shepherd over in Clachan was saying he reckons there's a deal of it back of the hills waiting for wind or darkness to unload it on us.' Taking a cromach from beside the door he and Wee Ruari went trudging companionably through the snow.

Kirsty had of course realised that Euan Ally and Enac were likely to be just as unfamiliar with Christmas as she herself had once been and indeed as Jamie had been. Jamie, however, had become progressively more tolerant of, if not partial to, the relatively small celebration she and Wee Ruari had managed to contrive each year. She hoped perhaps Euan Ally and Enac would become equally tolerant. She'd mentioned nothing about Christmas to Enac, but one day when Euan Ally had called in and had found her involved in putting the first icing on the cake he'd taxed her, almost accusingly, 'It's way past time for you to be doing that surely? Wee Ruari's birthday was a while ago, surely.'

He was accustomed to seeing her ice cakes for her son's birthday each year but, as he'd always managed to be with his folks in Clachan for the Hogmanay period, he had never before spent Christmas on Westisle.

'This one's for Christmas,' she'd explained, and in answer to his baffled look she'd told him, 'It's a week before Hogmanay just, but it's an English festival. I believe they have special church services and carol singers go round to the houses and then there's feastings with turkey and something like our black bun but they call it Christmas pudding. They have a cake and the children get presents from someone dressed up and called Father Christmas and they have parties in their houses and a tree decorated with baubles.'

He'd still looked puzzled. 'What like of parties?' he'd asked. 'Are they as good as our Halloween with dancing and such?'

'I wouldn't know; I've never been to one myself,' Kirsty admitted, 'but the shops were getting to take notice of some kind of event round about that time, but I thought it was coming up to Hogmanay just.'

'I've never known of such a thing,' he'd said disparagingly.

'Indeed, I'd never even heard of it myself till I was in Glasgow and working in the boarding house. I got used to hearing the occasional English visitors telling one another about happenings at Christmas-time and it all sounded so much fun that after Wee Ruari was born I thought I'd try and tell him about what I'd heard of an English Christmas so he'd know what to expect if he ever went there.'

'Ach, me and Enac have never been brought up to such things,' Euan Ally had been unimpressed. 'Halloween and the good times at Hogmanay were excitements enough for us and always have been.' He pulled on his jacket. 'I'd best be away then.'

Shortly before Christmas however, he'd arrived with a large cockerel already plucked and dumped it on the table. 'Enac says I'm to tell you that should help with your Christmas feastings, and she's making a good big dumpling ready for Hogmanay.' He'd left so hastily that she'd hardly had time to thank him.

With Jamie and Wee Ruari out of the way, Kirsty started preparing the Christmas dinner. The cockerel went into the oven, a large turnip went into the biggest pan, the potatoes scrubbed of their covering of earth into another one. The black bun, mixed and wrapped in a well boiled flour sack joined the cockerel in the oven, and while they were cooking she brought in the greenery from outside. By the time Jamie and Wee Ruari had returned, the kitchen was already redolent with smells of fresh greenery and savoury food.

'My! My! But this place is kind of shouting a welcome to anybody that's near it. I believe the gulls themselves are wanting in for a bite,' Jamie exclaimed as he divested himself of his oilskin.

Kirsty was adding the decorative coconut kisses to the icing on the cake at the time and Wee Ruari, arms on the table, was almost drooling at the sight.

'And what of Enac and Euan Ally?' she demanded.

'Ach, they'd like fine to come,' Jamie assured her. 'I reckon they'll be here in a wee whiley. Euan Ally was back from his sheep and Enac had only the hens to feed just.'

Wrestling with what seemed to be a deep pocket in his jacket, he triumphantly produced a bottle of whisky and then two bottles of Irn-Bru which he set on the table.

Kirsty's brows rose in astonishment. 'You didn't get those out on the moor,' she accused.

'No indeed. I got them the last time I was on the mainland but I've managed to keep them from himself here till now.' He tousled the boy's hair as he spoke.

Wee Ruari squeaked with delight as he saw the bottles of Irn-Bru.

'My, but aren't you the lucky one today?' Kirsty complimented her son who had by now found the bag of shortbread shapes and was already opening it. 'And that's your new jersey,' she said, handing him the package. He tore off the wrapping, and pulled the jersey over his head, puffing out his chest the better to display the pattern.

'I'll take a drink now, I'm awful thirsty,' he said, reaching for a bottle of Irn-Bru.

'No, no, not now,' Kirsty reproved. 'Best wait till Enac and Euan Ally get here.'

'But Ally likes Irn-Bru,' Wee Ruari protested. 'He keeps it on the boat. He might be drinking it all if he gets the chance.'

'Indeed he might so,' Kirsty agreed easily. 'But I doubt he'll not drink much Irn-Bru seeing as there's whisky,' she soothed and, conscious of his disconsolate expression added, 'And does not the Good Book say we must offer food and drink to the stranger within our house?'

Wee Ruari's lips puckered. 'Ally's no stranger,' he muttered.

Kirsty and Jamie exchanged covert glances.

'Come you now and help me make a Christmas table to surprise Enac and Euan Ally,' Kirsty cajoled. 'You must mind that this will be the first time they will be having what we have come to call our Christmas dinner.'

When she arrived Enac enthusiastically praised the decorations, complimenting Kirsty on the attractiveness and the appetising smell of the food before joining Euan Ally and Wee Ruari at the table. Jamie opened the bottle of whisky along with one of the bottles of Irn-Bru for Wee Ruari and, as if by doing so he had uncorked a latent exhilaration, they were all raising their glasses and murmuring indiscriminate toasts before partaking of the grand but nevertheless mysterious feast several days before the more exciting time of Hogmanay.

After the meal had been cleared away, Euan Ally produced a mouth organ and began to play one or two Gaelic tunes; Enac, who had a lovely voice, encouraged them all to join her in singing. The evening steadily grew more festive.

'Will you no come and dance a step or two with me?' Enac urged Wee Ruari. A little reluctantly he rose and held her hand as they jigged about the kitchen where Jamie had moved chairs to clear a space, but the jigging had to cease when Enac rested her hands on her stomach and claimed she was too full of food to carry on.

'Ach, it's too full of babby you are, that's what you're saying,' taunted Euan Ally.

'Maybe, but I've eaten enough tonight to need to starve for a day or two,' Enac retorted.

Kirsty was suddenly shocked into realising how heavily pregnant Enac was.

'I reckon you'd best take a bed here for tonight and not go trudging back to the "Castle" through all that snow,' she advised. 'Maybe it will be a wee bit of a strain.'

'No, no indeed. We'd best get back. The bairn will not be ready to come for the best part of a month and the walk back is maybe what I need just. Tapadh leat all the same.'

Kirsty glanced at Euan Ally seeking his approval. He seemed unperturbed. 'Aye, right enough we'd best be getting back to our own bed,' he supported. 'If there's snow to come as they say maybe we'll not find it so easy to walk back in the morning.'

'Aye, that's wise enough,' put in Jamie. 'Everyone's reckoning on more snow and so long as you've got plenty peats to keep you warm you'll be safe enough in your own place.'

'And we'll not go empty bellied,' confirmed Enac. 'We've got the venison, and there's more than plenty of oatmeal and salt herring to tide us over a long while. And I've a dumpling that's big enough to feed both families for Hogmanay.'

'Only if you're sure you'll be all right,' Kirsty attempted to dissuade them.

'Surely,' said Euan Ally, helping Enac into her jacket and wrapping his own muffler round his neck. 'She'll likely be dancing her way back.'

'I'll be following you with a lantern the best part of the way,' Jamie reassured. 'I missed seeing one of the stirks earlier on so I want to make sure it's still around.'

There was a chorus of 'Oidhche mhaths' as the three of them set off into the silent night.

chapter twelve

Hardly were the celebrations of Christmas and Hogmanay over than the end of Wee Ruari's school holiday was signalled by the calendar and it was time for him to return to Clachan. Though Kirsty always felt a little dispirited when the time for her son's departure loomed close, he at least never seemed in any way reluctant to return to school. Quite evidently he looked forward to rejoining the other scholars. Down at the shore she gave last minute cautions and reminders while Jamie coaxed the outboard motor into life and, in no time at all it seemed, the *Katy* was spearing out into the Sound to the accompaniment of a number of cheerful farewells and unconstrained waving.

Back at the house Kirsty flopped down on her chair in the kitchen and poured herself a cup of tea from the still warm pot. Only then did she let herself be plagued by a feeling of disquiet over her son's future.

More than a year before Wee Ruari had been due to start school Jamie had once or twice hinted that the boy might not be getting enough opportunities to fraternise with other children. His hints had nudged her into an appraisal of the situation. She'd debated with herself whether or not she was perhaps being too possessive in keeping him alone on the island when he was clever enough to go to school but on reflection she had decided it would be as good for him to stay on Westisle until he'd reached the statutory age for starting formal education. He did meet other children she told herself, though her subconscious argued that it was only occasionally; such as when Clachan children had been allowed to accompany older relatives on a rabbit-shooting expedition, but then the seriousness of the event usually had meant that the youngsters were so well disciplined that any attempts at more than the most superficial acquaintance, were negated by overwhelming shyness on both sides.

There had never been any doubt in Kirsty's mind that her son was a happy child. It had never struck her that he might be suffering from a lack of companionship with others of his own age. He always responded happily to the teasing and leg pulling which he got in good measure from Jamie and Euan Ally. When he was alone he was forever absorbed in examining, inventing or discovering new interests. There were endless diversions which occupied his attention; his days were full of activity from the minute he woke up until the minute he went to his bed. Kirsty had not been able to bring herself even to consider that he might be missing companionship.

When the right time had come she herself had taken him across the Sound to Clachan to enrol at the school and had been immediately reassured by his meeting with the other scholars. During his first weekend at home so enthusiastic had he sounded about his new companions, about his teachers and about his first lessons, it was evident that starting school was for him the beginning of a great new adventure. She'd prayed it might always remain so.

But now she had to face the fact that Clachan School was a junior school only. So where would her son go after that? Wee Ruari was growing up and would have to go further afield to continue his education; she would likely be separated from him not for one week or even two or three in rough weather but for whole terms. She was aware that wealthy people often chose to send their children to boarding schools from a very early age, but wealthy people she assumed were different; heartless perhaps, and their children likely hadn't experienced any close relationship with their mother. She put down her cup and scolded herself for her dreary introspection. After all, she reminded herself, island folks through the ages had had to leave home to pursue their interests, some to make their fortunes in one way or another. She must condition herself to accepting whatever might transpire. She rinsed her cup, swung the kettle over to the hob and went out to the barn to start filling sacks of hay ready for Jamie to take to the cattle when he returned from his trip to Clachan.

The snow had settled thickly on the ground, but the wind had eased and there was virtually no drifting. A heavy frost, however, had fashioned icicles to fringe the roof and sills of the house and similarly the tarpaulins and ropes that covered the haystack; crystal daggers hung from overhanging rocks and patches of sphagnum moss broke crisply underfoot.

When Jamie returned from Clachan he threw a tartan-wrapped box onto the table. 'That's from Mhairi Jane,' he explained. 'She reckons she's been sent that many boxes of shortbread for New Year she'll still be eating it at this time next year.'

Kirsty smiled. 'You can't have too many city relatives that can get to the shops when it comes to New Year,' she said. Opening the box she told Jamie to help himself. Taking a handful, he stuffed them into his pockets.

'They'll see me to the cattle,' he acknowledged, and was about to go out when there was a stamping of booted feet outside and a voice hailed them. The next moment Euan Ally pushed open the door and came into the kitchen, seeming unusually agitated.

'Why Euan Ally,' Kirsty exclaimed. 'It's not trouble that brings you surely.'

'It's herself,' he burst out between hurried breaths. 'The bairn came last night. Sooner by far than she reckoned.'

Kirsty blinked in astonishment. 'You're no after telling me Enac's dropped her baby, surely? It wasn't to be for another month or so.' Her tone was edged with incredulity, but since his expression was reassuring she rushed on, 'Tell me now what kind of a bairn would it be? A wee laddie just, or a lassie?' She poured a cup of tea and pushed it towards him.

'A wee laddie just, and not so wee either,' he told her proudly.

Jamie got up, shook Euan Ally's hand warmly and, after a few congratulatory words, produced the whisky bottle. Pouring out two generous measures he looked at Kirsty enquiringly but she shook her head.

'I'll take a dram to wet the baby's head at the proper time, when I see him,' she excused herself. 'And the bairn's fine, and Enac?' she continued.

'I'd say so. He's making more noise than a flock of hungry gulls already, I reckon I could hear him half-way to here.' He tossed off his whisky and gulped down a mouthful of tea.

'I'd say that was a good sign to be going on with,' Kirsty approved. 'I'd best be getting my boots on and get ready to go and take a look at Enac. Did you make sure she was all right before you left the house?'

'Indeed I did. She was taking the strupak I made for her and telling me to bring in more peats for the fire when I left. I reckon it was that easy for her you'd think she'd dropped a dozen bairns.'

'I doubt there's little enough would fash Enac,' Kirsty admitted, as she pulled on a coat and tied an old oilskin over it.

'Right,' she directed Euan Ally. 'Now I'm ready to go along with you.'

Quickly he drained his cup and reached for his cromach. Jamie had the door open, and the three of them stood together assessing the bleak snow-blanketed moors. It was a gentle enough day with a fold of pearl-grey cloud lying supinely across the hills, their white peaks appearing above it like newly awakened sleepers peering over the bedclothes.

'I'd best be away to the cattle I reckon,' said Jamie. He produced a couple of cromachs and handed one of them to Kirsty. 'You'd best take that,' he advised, 'though I'll surely be there to see you back.'

Kirsty started to protest but Euan Ally cut in, 'He has to come and take a dram with us anyway. Enac will not rest easy if he's not there to wet the bairn's head with her.'

'I'm not likely to miss that for certain sure,' was Jamie's retort as he turned towards the barn to collect the sacks of hay.

'And throw the hens an extra scoop of corn to see them right in case I don't get back before dark,' Kirsty called after him.

Euan Ally strode out, clumping forward through the snow; Kirsty kept behind him, following in his tracks.

'It's kind of soon yet, but has Enac spoken of naming the wee bairn?' she asked him.

'Indeed she has that,' he replied. 'I believe she's after naming him for an uncle she has in Australia somewhere.'

His voice sounded a little tetchy she thought, and she decided not to bother him with further questions. After all, she remembered, there were numerous uncles on both sides of the family and he and Enac might have had different ideas as to whom the child should be named for. She looked across the Sound, unusually calm and sunlit and doing its best to reflect the snowy peaks of the mainland hills which stood out sharply against the blue-washed serenity of the sky. The sight was so breathtaking she felt compelled to comment.

'It's a fortunate child to be born on an island surrounded by such beauty.'

Euan Ally paused for a moment. 'Aye indeed. It's no so bad here as it could be,' he acknowledged.

Kirsty found herself humming a favourite tune as they trudged along, and a moment later Euan Ally joined in.

'I'm gey surprised you have enough breath to sing,' he challenged her after a while.

'Just about enough,' she admitted. 'But you're setting the pace, and you don't seem that short of breath yourself.'

'Me? I've raced over the moors that was more thicker with snow than this, and with a full-grown ewe tied to my back and her newborn lamb in my arms,' he claimed, increasing his pace unwittingly as if the memory urged him on. Kirsty no longer had breath left to hum.

She managed to keep up with him nevertheless until they came in sight of his 'Castle'. The lowly cottage seemed to have snugged itself even deeper into the wintry moorland, looking as if it had belonged there for many years. Euan Ally halted and turned to her with a profoundly satisfied smile. She smiled back at him saying, 'Aye well, we've made it.'

He darted forward shouting loudly and moments later it seemed, he was pushing open the door of the cottage and shepherding Kirsty inside where a welcoming Enac sat beside the glowing range, a shawl-wrapped bundle in her arms.

'Well, well, and haven't you sprung a surprise on us,' Kirsty greeted Enac as she bent to kiss her.

'Indeed and didn't I surprise myself,' Enac acknowledged. 'Here's me not expecting the bairn to arrive until well after Hogmanay and now he's here at my breast.'

She lifted the shawl that was almost obscuring the baby's face so that Kirsty could get a good look at the new arrival.

'I must admit I was noticing him kicking around a bit stronger these last few days but now I believe with so much happening I likely let the months slip by me. But he's come and he's welcome and being early will mean I can get back to my loom that much sooner.'

'He's a bonny bairn right enough,' murmured Kirsty admiringly, 'and hasn't he a great look of Euan Ally about him just?'

'Indeed that's just the way I was thinking myself,' Enac responded.

'I'm away to the hill then,' Euan Ally called, and the two women continued their adulatory conversation while the child lay quietly against Enac's breast. Kirsty busied herself making the always compulsory and always acceptable cup of tea.

'I reckon you will have a name for him,' she probed.

'Aye, that's true enough,' admitted Enac. 'We're after saying we'll name him Adam for an uncle of mine that went out to Australia and made a deal of money. He was my mother's brother and she used to get a fair sum from him every year for her birthday. When I wrote to him telling of her death he sent a wee note, but he had no liking at all for my father so he sent no more money. I believe he's still a bachelor and has no family of his own to be named for him. Likely he'll be more than pleased to hear we have a bairn that we're going to name for him. A man likes to think he's remembered by his family no matter how far he is away and no matter how long he's been out of touch with them.' Carefully she settled the baby in the cradle.

'Maybe he'll come over from Australia to take a wee peep at the bairn,' Kirsty suggested.

'Aye, maybe so,' agreed Enac. 'It would be a long enough way but he'd be sure of a good welcome.'

Euan Ally, back from the hill, came into the kitchen, and immediately poured himself a cup of tea.

'And how's the wee mannie doing?' he asked, going over to the cradle, cup in hand.

'He's grand just,' Kirsty extolled. 'Really grand.'

'Take care with that tea!' cautioned Enac. 'I wouldn't want that you would drop a wee spot on his shawl.'

Obediently Euan Ally put his cup on the table. He opened a cupboard in the dresser from which he took out a bottle of whisky and four glasses. 'It's time we got round to wetting the bairn's head,' he enjoined.

'Oh, but the light will soon begin to fade,' Kirsty protested, glancing anxiously out of the window. 'I must surely be thinking of taking myself back.'

'Ach, there'll be a good moon tonight, and Jamie will surely be here in a wee whiley,' he assured her, pouring out a small whisky and handing it to her. She waved him away. 'Ach, take a wee one now and you'll be welcome to take another as soon as Jamie's here,' he pressed her.

'No I will not,' she demurred. 'We'll wet the bairn's head the way it should be done with us all here together. Is that not the way you would wish Enac?'

'Ach, there's plenty,' said Euan Ally, putting the glass to his own lips.

'Will I not clean some potatoes and set them in a pot beside the fire,' Kirsty volunteered. 'And maybe I could mix you an oatcake or a scone till Jamie gets here.'

'There's potatoes washed and in the pan,' Euan Ally assured her. 'Enac told me to do that before I came over to tell you about the bairn.' He picked up a bucket and went outside.

'And there's plenty scones and oatcakes in the meal bin waiting to be eaten,' added Enac. 'You sit and take another wee strupak and wait for Jamie.'

There was a faint noise from the baby and Enac put a hand on the cradle and gently rocked it. 'It's a grand cradle,' she commented admiringly.

For a moment Kirsty's breath caught in her throat. Enac's remark had twanged a memory so poignant it was like a sudden sting as, once again, she was assailed by the recollection of the degree of heartache that must have been endured by the man who had fashioned the cradle with such loving care. Time had helped Kirsty to grow a kind of carapace over the anguish of his passing but a chance remark, such as Enac's casual admiration of the cradle, could still jerk open the wound. She forced herself to take a deep breath and then to take a sip of tea before she managed to say evenly, 'Aye, and it's a grand bairn it's cradling.' Her eyes stared blankly at the small uncurtained window, not seeing the moonlit moorland.

There came the sound of voices from outside and a moment later Euan Ally pushed open the door to announce, 'Here comes Jamie boy and he's keen enough to wet the bairn's head with us. Is that not the way of it, Jamie?'

Enac got up immediately and filled the teapot from the simmering kettle while the two lads stood grinning as they flapped the snow from their caps and jackets. Euan Ally reached for the four glasses, filling each of them with whisky; together they toasted the bairn's head joyously, Euan Ally and Jamie quickly swallowing the first of the 'wetting', refilling their glasses ready for the toast of 'a long life to the bairn'. Euan Ally waved the bottle invitingly at the two women but Enac had been more restrained and had some whisky left; Kirsty had merely sipped hers, though she had echoed the toast heartily.

'You'd best drink it down,' Jamie instructed after a minute or two. 'We don't want to waste too much time before we start back.'

Kirsty added the rest of her drink to the tea left in her cup and drank it quickly, suppressing a shudder. 'I'm not keeping you back now,' she insisted, reaching for her overcoat.

Jamie managed to swallow another dram as they said their 'Oidhche mhaths' and then they were out in the snow.

'It's a grand night just,' Jamie remarked, looking up at the moonlit sky. 'I believe if the boat wasn't laid up for the winter me and Euan Ally would be talking of casting a net.'

Kirsty shuddered at the chilliness of the idea. 'For what?' she asked.

'Ach, a few tiddlers just,' Jamie replied nonchalantly.

'It would have been talk just, I'm thinking,' Kirsty summed up as she plodded behind him.

It was indeed a beautiful night. The full moon was sheening the water of the Sound and silvering the peaks of the hills. The still silence was broken only by the distant splashings of the tide, their own footsteps and the two cromachs crunching in the snow. Jamie appeared to be preoccupied and Kirsty was tight-lipped against the cold in case it should provoke an ache in a sensitive tooth she had. Pulling her beret down over her ears as far as it would reach and tucking her chin into the collar of her overcoat she followed Jamie's footsteps.

When they reached the house Jamie volunteered to close up the hens. Kirsty set about replenishing the fire and swinging the kettles over the hob. Both kettles were steaming by the time Jamie came into the kitchen.

'I'll make us a strupak and then we can see what we need before we take to our beds,' she greeted him. He ignored her and, going to the cupboard, brought out the whisky bottle.

'I'll take a dram or two before I say what I want,' he told her.

She regarded him with raised eyebrows.

'I should have thought you'd had plenty of drams this night,' she taxed him.

'Nothing like a wee dram to keep out the cold,' he assured her. 'Will you no take one to warm you?' He set two glasses on the table.

'Not for me,' she insisted. 'I don't pretend to like the stuff and a cup of tea will warm me better than whisky.'

'Suit yourself,' he said, shrugging his shoulders. He flopped down on the bench, his eyelids lowering as his head drooped forward. She herself was tired and not particularly hungry. She brought out the remains of a fruit dumpling and put it on the table and, after pouring herself a mug of tea, she cut a thick slice. She turned to look enquiringly at Jamie and realised that he was fast asleep. Deciding against wakening him, she ate her dumpling, drank her tea and, reckoning that he would very likely sleep until daylight, left the food on the table in case he should wake and feel hungry. Piling more peats on the fire, she turned down the lamp though knowing it would likely burn itself out before morning. She went to her bed, feeling only slightly uneasy at the thought of all the day's chores which the birth of Enac's bairn had prevented her from doing.

chapter thirteen

In the night the wind rose, besetting the land, and by morning a full gale was flinging the accumulations of snow haphazardly so that, day after day, they found themselves struggling almost blindly against the storm; Kirsty only as far as the hen-house and back; Jamie often floundering over the moors to and from the cattle.

'Ach, they don't wander so much in this kind of weather,' he'd commented when she had tried to commiserate with him. 'I'm not needing to search for them in a different place each day like in the summer.'

'And Euan Ally?' she enquired.

'His sheep are feeding in the bluebell glen or thereabouts. He's not missing any so far as I know.'

Week after week the storm raged with the occasional lull lasting only long enough to delude them into thinking that the worst was over before it returned with increased vigour, tearing the thick clouds out of the sky and leaving it, when darkness came, rigid with starshine. At length it subsided to a petulant breeze and soon they were rewarded with a gentle evening when the serrated outline of the hills was gradually absorbed by the deepening twilight until they were at one with the night. Kirsty and Jamie began to consider what the next bout of work must be.

'I reckon the spring will come early this year,' Jamie prophesied confidently.

'It can't come too early for me,' Kirsty opined. 'The winter's been pretty coarse.' They were standing outside the house and from habit were assessing the sea. After a pause she felt compelled to ask, 'Would you be reckoning on getting across to Clachan this week?' She hadn't seen her son for six weeks and was feeling his absence.

'Aye, I reckon the *Katy* will be making the trip so we'll get Wee Ruari home for the weekend surely.'

Kirsty's mouth relaxed into a thankful smile. It would be good to hear her son's chatter as a change from the roaring of the waves.

True to Jamie's prophecy, the signs of spring soon began to manifest themselves. Jamie and Euan Ally decided the time was right to start getting *The Two Ruaris* sorted and ready for sea. Then one of the hens started to go broody. It was too early according to Enac, who advised her to follow the accepted practice of putting the hen into a sack and hanging it from a line where it would be well buffeted by the wind. With no place to settle or roost the hen would get over its broodiness within a couple of days and would be ready to start laying again. Kirsty chose to ignore her advice however and set a clutch of eggs under the hen.

Once *The Two Ruaris* was sorted 'the boys' made the trip to the mainland and Jamie brought back a message from Dogan to remind her that the time was getting on for a muirburn.

'Already?' Kirsty queried.

'Aye, I reckon he's right enough. We could be doing with an extra hand or two so maybe when I go for Wee Ruari I'll talk to a couple of the Clachan lads and see if they're willing.'

He reported that the men would indeed be prepared to help 'after the Sabbath' – a condition which Wee Ruari protested against since it meant that the muirburn would take place when he was back at school.

'You'll get a much better sight of it from Clachan,' Kirsty told him. 'You'll be able to see the island ringed with fire!'

The boy was not prepared to be comforted however. 'I'd sooner be here,' he argued sulkily but since Monday morning dawned calm there was no excuse for him to remain on the island instead of going to school.

Once the muirburn was finished the urgency of the season's work began to assert itself and, on a day attended by a 'pride of the morning mist' that was reckoned to foretell a spell of fine weather, Kirsty was turning the sheets she had washed and spread out on the dyke the previous evening when she heard Enac hailing her.

'I see you're busy then.'

'Aye, I was wanting to get these turned while the dew was still on them,' she acknowledged. 'You yourself are about early enough. And what news of the wee one just?'

Turning to show Kirsty the 'wee one' tucked snug and safe in the shawl she wore across her shoulders Enac nodded approvingly.

'My mother always said May was the month for bleaching,' she agreed. 'The sun dries things too quickly when it comes later in the year.'

145

Kirsty surveyed the hills across the Sound, which, though they still looked taciturn, had shed their winter grimness.

'Aye, I believe the time's coming for a bit of blanket washing too,' she observed.

'Indeed, I myself have one or two blankets that could do with a wash,' said Enac, adjusting her shawl as the baby wriggled. 'They belonged to my mother so I brought them over with the loom. You mind you were after saying there was a good burn for blanket washing over-by,' she nodded her head towards her cottage.

'I do indeed mind saying that,' Kirsty admitted.

'Well, if Euan Ally or Jamie will carry over the nice big tub you have here we could make a day of it together,' suggested Enac. 'May is best for blanket washing too, I mind.'

Kirsty led the way into the house where the kettle was simmering on the fire. She glanced closely at Enac as she handed her a strupak; the girl seemed a little perturbed she thought and to be paying more than usual attention to the baby.

'The bairn's not worrying you?' she asked anxiously.

'No, no indeed,' refuted Enac. 'He's a right broth of a boy. If I'm worried it's because of a letter I got in the post and Euan Ally says I must ask you about it before I reply.'

'Is it something to do with me then?' Kirsty enquired.

'Well, it is and it isn't in a kind of way,' admitted Enac. 'It's this way. When we went to stay with my sister for our wedding this lassie called. She had twin bairns, a boy and a girl maybe about five years old but well advanced both of them. Lovely bairns they were too and she was bringing them up to be right wee heroes. She was a nice enough lassie I thought, and married to a laughter-filled Irishman though I didn't know then that they were living in the Gorbals!'

Kirsty's lips tightened at the mention of the Gorbals, remembering the unsavoury stories of that area of blighted tenements and of those who lived there.

'Well, this Irish husband of hers,' Enac continued. 'She seemed happy enough with him, but it seems he got in with a gang of gamblers. He lost all his money, if he'd ever had any, then she found he hadn't being paying the rent and soon the bailliffs came and took away all the furniture save for a bed. Her man was sent to prison and then the landlord gave her no more than two weeks to find the rent money or she would have to get out. She might have been able to do it too for she got a shilling or two from an old woman for doing her washing and ironing and things, but when the children came home from school one day with tear-stained faces saying the other pupils had been taunting them that their father was in prison and they'd never see him again she couldn't stand it just. She had told them that he'd gone away to see about a job. Straightaway she set to and made sleeping bags for them and with their tent and what little money she had they took off for a farm where they used to go camping. But when they got there they found that the farmer had died and the farm had been sold. She didn't know the new people, but they said she could camp there for a couple of weeks. My sister kept in touch with her, and now she writes to me to ask can they come to the island where they won't be known and camp on Euan Ally's croft for a little while?' She looked at Kirsty enquiringly. 'Euan Ally doesn't mind, but he says I must ask you first.'

'Ach, the poor soul! Of course I don't mind.' Kirsty's voice was edged with compassion.

'She's no island girl,' Enac sounded a note of caution.

Kirsty smiled. 'She doesn't have to be an island girl to pitch a tent on Westisle for a couple of weeks, does she?'

'No, but what I'm saying is she won't be used to our way of doing things. She'll be a townie more than likely.'

'Well, we'll have to show her won't we,' Kirsty rejoined, and saw the look of relief that came over Enac's face.

' "The boys" are after saying they're reckoning to make a trip to the mainland tomorrow to collect a pile of wood so I'll be sure to try to get word to her telling her she's welcome to come and camp on the island.' Enac seemed to be assuring herself of her intention.

That same evening Jamie carried the washtub to the burn by the 'Castle' and the next day the two women trod the blankets with their bare feet in the soapy water and then stretched them in the burn, securing them with a few suitably sized boulders, to rinse in the fast flowing water. Afterwards they both sat on the bank wiggling their feet in the water while Enac's baby slept peacefully in the cradle beside them.

'I mind my granny saying that this was the best part of the yearly blanket washing,' Kirsty told Enac. 'She reckoned it did more good to her corns than anything else.'

'I'll mind that when I come to get corns,' Enac responded. 'But right now I'm ready for a strupak.'

Together they picked up the cradle and, still barefoot, carried it back to the cottage.

'That's one good job jobbed as my mother used to say,' Enac remarked as she brewed a pot of tea and filled a couple of mugs.

Kirsty nodded. 'The first of the spring jobs,' she agreed as she drank her tea.

'I'll be over in the evening to help get the blankets on the dyke to dry,' she promised Enac as she pulled on her stockings and boots ready to start back. 'And I'll bring you the *Bulletin* to have a read of. I forgot to bring it with me this morning.'

'I'll look forward to that,' replied Enac. The *Bulletin* was the only paper 'the boys' could manage to get hold of when they went to the mainland, and every word of it was read, even the advertisements. Kirsty particularly liked the recipes; Enac liked to read of the goings on in all the various districts and, since every scrap of paper was precious and had to be conserved for one purpose or another, parts of the *Bulletin* often lay about the house for weeks at a time.

The baby whimpered. 'He lets me know soon enough when he wants feeding,' said Enac as she bared her breast.

When *The Two Ruaris* returned from the mainland the next day 'the boys' brought with them not only a load of wood but, to Enac's astonishment, a woman and two children along with their camping gear. Kirsty was not there to see them land and the first she heard of the new arrivals was from Jamie.

'However did that come about?' she asked in astonishment. 'Enac was to give you a letter to post to the woman telling her she would be welcome to come and set up a tent for a couple of weeks and yet here they are before a letter could possibly have got to them.'

149

'Aye, well it seems the woman was offered a lift to the port by a lorry driver she knew that was coming to collect fish. She went into the post office to ask if there was any place she might pitch a tent for the night and happened to mention that she knew someone from Westisle. The postmistress told her *The Two Ruaris* was in the harbour that very day and maybe she would get a chance to go and see her friend. Well, while they were talking Euan Ally came in to buy a stamp to put on Enac's letter. The postmistress told him that the woman there knew Enac and when they began talking and Euan Ally realised who the woman was he gave her the letter to save the stamp. When the woman had read the letter she started to cry and told Euan Ally that Enac had said she would be welcome to camp on Westisle. Well, Euan Ally didn't think that Enac would be too pleased if he left them there so he told them to get aboard the boat there and then. So here they are. Enac was knocked back with surprise when she saw them, but she's looking after them for now until they can get the tent up.'

It was not until the following day that Kirsty met the woman and her two children. An embarrassed Enac introduced the equally embarrassed mother as Marney and the twins as Julie and Johnny. They were a shy but well-behaved trio she thought, and wondered how Wee Ruari would react to having strange children on the island. Since the next day was a Friday and the sea looked placid enough she had no doubt that Jamie would be bringing her son home from school and she was likely to find out soon enough.

They were all down at the shore to meet the *Katy* the following afternoon, and as soon as Wee Ruari stepped from the boat Enac called out.

'Here you are Ruari, we've got two children for you to look after and teach.'

Kirsty thought her son stared at the twins disapprovingly; it was his customary reaction when meeting strangers and the twins sidled behind their mother.

'They're awful wee,' was her son's comment after he had met them. 'Not nearly so big as me.'

'You're older than them,' she pointed out.

'Are they going to stay here?'

'Until their father comes to collect them.'

'Where will they go then?'

'Back to Glasgow, I suppose.' She hoped he would not question the children about their father's whereabouts.

His curiosity satisfied he went on to tell her, 'There are touries in Clachan.'

'Touries already?' she was surprised.

'Mhairi Beag has two staying with her this week and she says she has two booked for next week.'

'She'll be pleased enough at that.'

They were sitting in the kitchen and Jamie, having taken off one of his seaboot socks, was inspecting it as if he suspected a thorn or a piece of crab shell had lodged in the foot of it.

'I think someone's been putting cockle shells in my socks,' he accused lightly, looking at Wee Ruari.

'No, it was a whelk shell,' the boy teased, backing away as if he was dodging a clout.

'I'll whelk you if you try it,' threatened Jamie.

'You mean you'll skelp me, don't you?'

151

'Both,' retorted Jamie, making a swipe in the boy's direction. There followed a jovial altercation as Jamie put on his sock and stamped his foot into his boot.

'I'm thinking you'll maybe be getting some touries over here for yourself in a few weeks,' he told Kirsty.

'Here? On Westisle?'

Jamie nodded confirmation.

'Are you after thinking you'll be ready for them?' he asked her.

'Have you ever known me to be any other way?' She pretended to be indignant.

'No, I mean for them to stay in the house here,' he insisted.

'Haven't I got plenty potatoes and oatmeal and eggs and rabbits and milk...'

'Ach, there's no need to go on. You know very well what I'm meaning.' He sounded slightly testy. 'Can I let you know within half an hour of knowing myself just?'

She nodded solemnly then, seeing his tight-set mouth, she smiled. 'Half an hour will be time enough,' she assured him, while making a mental note to begin airing the two beds in the loft.

As the weather grew more settled, and Wee Ruari was home for the summer holidays, Kirsty saw more of the twins who were soon being chaperoned about the island by her son. He did not seem to mind their presence while they apparently felt privileged to be in his company. The change in them was remarkable; their cheeks exchanged paleness for a rosier hue, their legs grew visibly sturdier and even their shyness moderated to such an extent that Kirsty could now speak to them without them hanging their heads and feigning dumbness.

It was over a strupak that she and Enac were discussing with Marney the difference in the children – their increasing robustness, their growing confidence – as they watched Wee Ruari show them how to build suitably shaped stones into a sturdy dyke.

'Oh, they love being here,' enthused Marney, and Kirsty caught the touch of regret in her tone. 'To them it's a great adventure.'

'Bairns are bound to love the island,' said Enac confidently. 'Or they do until they get to thinking there's a more exciting life elsewhere.' Looking down at her baby nestled in its shawl she continued complacently. 'Likely that'll not be bothering me for a whiley yet though.'

'Only another year for me," lamented Kirsty. 'Wee Ruari will have to go further afield then I reckon.'

'He'll be ready for it,' Enac comforted.

'He'll be ready enough,' Kirsty agreed, 'but it's not something I'll be looking forward to just the same.'

'My two would like fine to go to Wee Ruari's school in Clachan,' put in Marney. 'So they say anyway.'

Enac murmured a disinterested, 'Aye', but Kirsty forbore comment.

'How long could they be thinking of staying on the island with only a tent for a home?' she asked herself.

Jamie had confided that, according to Euan Ally, in inclement weather the ever hospitable, ever generous Enac insisted that the visitors bring their sleeping bags into the kitchen of the 'Castle'. Euan Ally grumbled that this was inconvenient when it was an early morning start for the fishing. In fact Euan Ally had said that he was becoming fearful that if they stayed much longer he would be relegated to a bunk in the loom shed so that Marney could share Enac's bed. Kirsty quelled a faint sense of guilt at her own attitude and deemed it wiser to deflect the conversation.

'Jamie was after telling me to be expecting touries to stay before long,' she disclosed after a suitable silence had elapsed.

'Aye, I believe that professor is already in Clachan and staying with his daughter at Morag's,' Enac acknowledged. 'Euan Ally reckons they'll be wanting over here now they know you have a couple of rooms to let. It seems they found plenty to take their fancy when they were over for the day that time.'

'They seemed well satisfied with their visit,' Kirsty allowed.

It was only a few days later that Jamie announced, 'If the sea is calm enough in the morning I'll be bringing over the Canadian professor and his daughter that was here last summer; they're wanting to stay on the island for a week or two.'

'For a week or two!' She was surprised, not because they were coming, but by the proposed length of their stay. 'As long as that?' she queried.

Jamie looked at her defiantly as if challenging her to protest. She remained silent, merely comforting herself that the beds would be well and truly aired.

The morning was calm when Jamie set off for Clachan and Kirsty made sure to be on the shore to welcome the expected guests.

'You look well,' she greeted them, shaking hands warmly.

'We feel on top of the world,' responded Hugh Roberton. 'We've been visiting various islands and the weather's been really kind to us.'

'Oh yes, indeed,' confirmed Dina. 'We've been swimming with seals and stroking porpoises and, while I've been searching for specimens, Pop's been searching for long-lost relatives.' She turned to Jamie and Kirsty noticed the depth and warmth of the smile they exchanged.

'And did you trace any relatives?' Kirsty asked Hugh Roberton.

'No,' he admitted. 'But we met an old man who used to live on the island of Killegray and he believes my mother came from there. It's hard to find out any more for Killegray was evacuated some years ago, and apart from a few sheep no one lives there any more.'

'I did hear that right enough,' Kirsty agreed, remembering how shocked she had been to read of the folks she had known deserting their island; the island where she had been born and where she had lived with her Granny and Uncle Donny until her Granny had died and she had been sent to the city to live with an elderly aunt. She'd hated the thought of the friendly little community being disbanded; of the lovely little island left without the varied activities, the sounds and smells of people to sustain it. She'd hoped to go back to it some day and make a home there; a home for herself and Uncle Donny... But the hope had been killed by city life.

'Did you get a name for the old man you met?' she enquired.

'I think he said that he was a Calum McRae but he didn't seem too sure about it. He was answering to "Ally" and

155

even "Shorus" so I think he was pretty mixed up in his mind.'

Kirsty summoned her memories. The postman on Killegray had been called Calum or 'Calum the post'; 'Calum McRae' she had never heard of, for there were no surnames used on Killegray. But 'Calum the post' would be very old by now she reckoned, and even had he still been alive she was certain that he would never have agreed to be evacuated from his home. She made no mention of her recollections to Hugh Roberton for it seemed to her unlikely that his forebears hailed from her own small community and she had no wish to disappoint him.

By this time they had reached the house where Jamie carried the bags up the stairs. Euan Ally arrived with Enac and the baby and Marney. Wee Ruari ushered in the twins, and after greetings and introductions and sessions of admiration for the baby, Euan Ally eventually said, 'You'll surely be coming over to the "Castle" to see how comfortable we are.'

'Oh yes Pop, why don't we do just that,' Dina responded eagerly but as she moved to get up her father handed her a carrier bag.

'You've forgotten this,' he reminded her.

'So I have. Look Wee Ruari, we've brought you this.'

Dina handed him a square black tin of toffee. Kirsty had always known toffee as 'tablet' though they saw little enough of it unless 'the boys' brought some after a visit to the mainland. Wee Ruari beamed his thank yous; breaking off three pieces he gave one to each of the twins and kept one for himself. He then put the tin away in the cupboard of the dresser, for in his experience adults didn't eat toffee.

Hugh Roberton looked at Kirsty enquiringly.

'Will you be going over to this "Castle" with them?'
he asked.

'Not just now,' she replied. 'I have one or two things I
must do here. I'll be over there in a wee while just.'

'Then if you don't mind I'll wait here and go with you,'
he rejoined. 'You don't object to my pipe?'

When Kirsty indicated that she had no objection he
settled more comfortably on the bench, devoting himself
to getting his pipe drawing properly.

'Jamie and Euan Ally seem to be content with how
they're doing at the fishing,' he observed casually after a
few minutes. It sounded like a statement but there was
a query in his tone.

'Content enough,' she replied. 'Prices could be better.'

'How about the croft itself? They tell me in Clachan that
there's not much return on cattle and sheep these days.'

'There never has been as far as I can remember,' she
admitted.

'I suppose not,' he agreed. 'But once a man has worked
his own land he'll never want to leave it.' He puffed at his
pipe once or twice and then said, 'You know, in my
country they say that the land fashions the man. Would
you think so yourself?'

'And the sea?' she queried. 'My two husbands were
fishermen as well as crofters.'

Hugh Roberton raised his eyebrows.

'The sea rules a man,' she supplied, answering her
own question. 'You know it's said hereabouts that a true
fisherman who has his own boat belongs to the sea
completely. He has no need of other diversions such as a
wife and a home. If he has a wife she is an indulgence,
a luxury.'

157

He was still looking at her quizzically. 'You knew that before you were married?'

She nodded.

'But you accepted it?'

'I suppose I ignored it. Women do.'

'Is that what you would advise any young woman to do?'

'I cannot say. Myself I was not young when I married.'

Getting up quickly from her chair she put more peats on the fire and adjusted the position of the two kettles, hoping her apparent haste would end the discussion. She had no wish to tell him how her two marriages had come about.

'We'd best be getting over to the "Castle" or we'll meet them on their way back,' she urged.

He knocked out his pipe and rose to his feet. As he pulled on his jacket he taxed her. 'I take it you know something about the state of affairs between Dina and Jamie?'

'I can see they seem to be fond of each other,' she admitted.

'More than fond,' he returned. 'They claim to be in love and are planning to get married.'

The shock of his statement was almost physical.

'Jamie and Dina? But they hardly know each other,' she protested.

'They've been corresponding regularly since that first day we spent over here.' He was smiling at her now.

'I didn't know of that,' she said simply. 'It is Jamie who collects the mail.'

'Yes, I gathered that,' he murmured sympathetically then, noticing her perplexed frown, he demanded, 'You're not pleased?'

'I have no reason to be unpleased,' but her voice made him turn to her quickly.

'No, don't feel that way,' he begged her. 'I strongly suspected but I didn't know myself until we were on the island of Killegray a week or two ago. I managed to get the truth out of her then just how serious things had become.'

'I've always hoped Jamie would meet a nice girl who would return his love for her and want to marry him,' she reflected. 'I was sure it would happen some day but he didn't seem to fancy any of the lassies he met hereabouts. I didn't want him to end up a bachelor like too many of the men in these parts; he's too kind and gentle and thoughtful. I know he'll make a good husband when he marries.'

'Perhaps Dina is the right girl for him,' Hugh Roberton said softly.

'Oh I hope you're right,' Kirsty exclaimed, smiling. 'She is a lovely girl. I couldn't wish him better.'

'She'll be glad to know that,' he returned.

When they reached the 'Castle' they found Dina cuddling Enac's baby, Enac showing Marney how to card wool and the twins and Wee Ruari fishing in the burn. Jamie and Euan Ally watched Hugh Roberton inspect the stonework of the walls before taking him inside to see the new range and the loom where a length of tweed was already in the process of being woven. When they reappeared they declared their intention of inspecting the sheep, and Dina, parting reluctantly with the baby, decided to accompany them.

'Euan Ally's Uncle Hamish says he is coming over in a day or two to start building up a bothy for the English couple.' Enac imparted the information with a satiric grin, and went on 'His old wife is letting him off the rope again for a wee whiley.'

'So they managed to persuade him that they're serious,' Kirsty was still sceptical.

There was a sudden shout from the children down at the burn to come and see the size of the fish they had caught.

Marney dashed off to join them but Enac and Kirsty remained seated. As soon as Marney was out of earshot Enac spoke.

'I have to tell you Marney's husband will be here tomorrow. He's waiting at the port and the boys are going to pick him up after they've finished fishing.' After a pause she continued. 'He's served his sentence now.'

Kirsty nodded comprehendingly but made no comment.

' "The boys" say he can sleep on the boat for a night or two,' Enac offered.

'Is Marney looking forward to seeing him?'

'I reckon she is.'

'And the twins, will they be pleased?'

'They'll be over the moon, Marney says. They think the world of their father.'

'Ought we to provide some sort of welcome for him?' Kirsty wondered.

Enac pursed her lips by way of reply and Kirsty did not pursue the matter.

'There's something I have to tell you Enac,' she disclosed, 'and I think it will surprise you as much as it surprised me.' Enac turned to her questioningly, and Kirsty announced, 'I'm told Jamie and Dina are planning to get married.'

'Ah, the dears,' breathed Enac, smiling broadly.

'Is that all you have to say; I expected you to jump out of your skin.'

'I'm not very surprised,' Enac admitted and, seeing Kirsty's puzzled expression, she went on, 'I expected it in a way. Euan Ally's been mentioning all these letters Jamie's after getting with Canadian stamps on them, so I was pretty sure something was going on.'

'I feel a bit left out,' said Kirsty. 'I think I must have been wilfully blind but now I feel stupid just.'

'Did they tell you whereabouts they are going to make their home?' Enac's question shocked her.

'Their home!' Kirsty turned away quickly so Enac should not see her startled expression. 'No, they haven't spoken to me of their plans. It was Dina's father who told me of their intention to be wed.'

'I suppose they'll go to Canada to live,' Enac offered casually.

'I suppose that will be the way of it,' agreed Kirsty automatically, but as the realisation pierced sharply into her mind she had to smother her dismay. She was glad of the distraction as Wee Ruari and the twins came racing up to them to show off the fish they had caught.

'My, but that's a fine trout you have there,' Enac complimented them as she inspected the fish. 'Today will be a day for you to remember.' Wee Ruari's smile broadened as he and the twins dashed off again.

And that's how he would remember the day, Kirsty told herself. Such things as calendars were alien to the islanders; they packed their memories with events which they would later call to mind clearly. Seasons needed no calendar; even the months were vague; the missionary or the minister would remind them of the days of Communion festivals and Hogmanay, so dates were of no consequence. 'I mind that was the day I caught the big trout in Euan Ally's burn,' she knew Wee Ruari would recall in later years, just as she might say, 'I mind that was the day Hugh Roberton told me of Jamie and Dina's secret,' or Enac might recollect, 'I mind it was the day before Marney's man came to the island.' And so the evocations would continue throughout the years. She herself kept a calendar in the house but it was only to mark off the days approaching Christmas so she could be sure of preparing some special treats for Wee Ruari.

'It's certainly been a day for memories,' she summed up. 'But I'd best be getting back and doing some work.'

She was glad to be alone; to wrestle with the tangle of emotions that filled her mind. The startling revelation that morning of the situation between Jamie and Dina had shaken her, but almost immediately she had welcomed it as she would have welcomed Dina into her home. Enac's assumption that the couple would probably wish to make their home in Canada had certainly unnerved her. She knew she must now come to grips with the likelihood that Jamie would desert Westisle and go with Dina to Canada, but even as she faced the facts questions pursued one another through her mind. If Jamie left would Euan Ally and Enac stay? What would happen to *The Two Ruaris?*

Her shoulders dropped listlessly and she paused to stare at the hills, white-flecked now with a scatter of newly shorn sheep. So Clachan had begun shearing! Her mind grasped the knowledge and then almost immediately let it slide away. Her eyes were drawn to the innumerable segments of white cloud that looked as if they might be tiny fish shoaling across the tranquil blue sky. She stiffened her shoulders and resumed her path until the memory of Marney's man smote her. Enac had said he would be arriving the following evening. What was to happen to him and his family? Was she to be confronted with more problems and even more decisions?

When she reached the house she found Wee Ruari and the twins scoffing pancakes and crowdie with cream.

'We were hungry,' they explained. 'So we thought we'd start with pudding and then we'll have the fish we caught.'

'So who's to cook the fish,' she teased. 'Are you going to try your hand at cooking it as well as eating it?'

They could see she wasn't serious, but Wee Ruari shook his head anyway. 'You can cook it,' he allowed. The three of them ran outside.

Jamie, Dina and her father arrived shortly afterwards and Dina sniffed appreciatively at the rabbit pie that was keeping warm on the hob.

'Mmm. I always seem to be hungry on this island,' she declared.

'Fresh air and good cooking,' agreed her father.

'I'm going to be missing Mam's cooking,' began Jamie and then broke off to stare guiltily at Kirsty.

She was putting the food onto their plates and the sudden confession caused her hand to shake so that the pie slid to one side, spilling gravy onto the wax-cloth covering. Quickly she seized a cloth and wiped it up.

'That was clumsy of me,' she excused herself.

No one commented. Wordlessly they began eating until Kirsty decided she must ease the tension. 'Dina's father is after telling me you two are planning to get married,' she challenged them.

163

Dina blurted out smilingly. 'We were intending to let you into the secret tonight, weren't we Jamie? Truly we were.'

Kirsty acknowledged her confession with a nod of approval. Looking at Jamie she saw his face was deeply flushed.

'I reckoned you might have picked up a hint of it,' he excused himself.

'Well I'm mighty pleased to hear of it,' she enthused, leaning forward to shake their hands. 'And now that's all said and done with, let's start on the pancakes and crowdie.'

Jamie got up and went to the larder, returning with a bottle from which he filled two large glasses and two small ones.

'This is by way of a celebration,' he invited.

At that moment Wee Ruari came in. 'That's whisky,' he accused.

'We're celebrating,' Jamie told him.

'Celebrating what?' her son asked.

The adults exchanged glances and nodded.

'Dina and me are engaged and are going to be wed,' Jamie explained.

'But Dina and her father are only here for a holiday, then they'll be going back to Canada,' argued Wee Ruari.

'Maybe I'll be going with them to take a look and see if it's as nice as Westisle,' Jamie hazarded.

'Why can't Dina stay here instead,' Wee Ruari suggested.

'Because I have to go back to college,' she answered.

'You don't have to go to Canada to go to college,' he told her knowledgeably. 'Finlay McIntosh from Clachan goes to college and he comes home nearly every weekend.'

'It's a different kind of college,' Jamie tried to explain, but Kirsty cut him short.

Feeling they might want her son out of the way for a while she urged, 'Ruari, away and close up the hens will you. There were a few hoodies about this morning.'

'Right enough,' agreed Jamie. 'And since we're going to the mainland tomorrow I'll bring you plenty of Irn-Bru so you and the twins can have lots of celebrations.'

Wee Ruari went a little reluctantly to close the poultry shed and by the time he came back Kirsty had cleared the table and they were all drinking tea or smoking. Squeezing onto the bench beside Dina he announced, 'If Jamie's going to Canada I'm going too.'

Jamie raised his eyebrows while Dina put an arm round the boy's shoulders. Kirsty puckered her lips.

'What, and leave your mother here?' Jamie asked sternly.

'No, she'll want to come too, you just ask her and you'll see.'

'Well, I'm asking her now so you can hear for yourself what she says.' It was Dina's father who spoke. 'She will be more than welcome.'

Kirsty saw that everyone was looking at her; she shook her head gravely.

'How can I go to Canada,' she asked lightly. 'A big house and cattle and everything to look after. I couldn't leave them here without me.'

'Euan Ally and Enac would look after them for you,' Wee Ruari put in insistently.

'I think we should all go to bed and think about Canada just,' Kirsty proposed, noticing that Dina was almost asleep on Jamie's shoulder. They all wished each other 'Oidhche mhath' and made their way towards their bedrooms.

Kirsty herself didn't want to think about Canada but it still impinged on her sleeplessness. Not the idea of her going there – that did not bear thinking about – but the dilemma she would be in when Jamie went. She tossed and turned as solution after solution formed in her mind only to be discarded as unsuitable.

chapter fourteen

When she entered the kitchen next morning Kirsty was surprised to see Jamie and Dina already up. Jamie had lit the fire, made the porridge and brewed the tea.

'I'm afraid I've slept a bit late,' she apologised.

'No, no, it's just that Dina is coming with us on the boat today to take a look at the port,' Jamie explained.

'Marney said yesterday that she would like to come too,' Dina put in. 'I believe her husband is arriving today and she wants to meet him.'

'I take it Wee Ruari's not awake yet, or I'm sure you would have another passenger,' Kirsty smiled gently.

In a short while they were away, leaving her to sit down to a quiet cup of tea, but it was not long before Hugh Roberton joined her.

'You know Dina says she gets the best cup of tea she's ever tasted here. She doesn't drink much tea at home since the usual drink in Canada is coffee. I guess we'll have to take some back with us.'

Kirsty smiled. 'I expect it's the water. I myself didn't think the tea they drink in the city was as good as it is on Westisle.'

'You were in the city quite a long time?'

167

'Quite a number of years,' she admitted. 'But I had a good employer.'

'And yet you were born on an island, so Jamie tells me.'

She took a deep breath to steady herself. 'I was born and lived with my granny on the very island you were speaking of, the Island of Killegray.'

He turned to her, astonished. 'You never mentioned that when we were speaking of it before.'

'I didn't see how your people could be from Killegray without my having some memory of them, but I had no wish to spoil your hopes. And although my mother was from the island, I never knew anything about my father save that he hailed from Glasgow. After I was born, my mother left me with my granny and emigrated. I never saw her again.'

Hugh Roberton was staring at her incredulously.

'Why so surprised?' she asked.

'Because my mother told my late wife that she'd had a child that she'd left with her own mother before she came to Canada. She said she intended to come back for the child but she never dared to tell my father. Surely there wouldn't be more than one such in a small community.'

Fraction by fraction, they were struggling to the inevitable conclusion.

'What name were you christened?' Hugh Roberton asked.

'I doubt I was ever christened,' she responded. 'Folks don't go much for that sort of thing in the islands. But my granny was a McLellan so that would have been my mother's maiden name; I was known as Kirsty McLellan.'

'My mother's maiden name was McLellan,' the words came from him haltingly. 'Is it possible that we are half-brother and sister?'

168

She was already well ahead of him and nodded slowly. 'It has crossed my mind that we might share the same mother.'

He stretched out a hand and grasped her wrist.

'That's it then. I've found my relative. It seems too good to be true.'

'Do you want to believe it?' she queried.

'Of course I want to believe that I've found the half-sister I've been seeking for such a long time. Can it be true that you and I are related?'

'I believe it to be true,' she assured him with a smile.

He smiled at her in return, but suddenly the excitement drained from his face.

'Is there something you do not like about the relationship between us?' she asked.

He rested his head on his arms. 'I guess I am not liking the thought of Dina and Jamie getting married now,' he admitted awkwardly.

'But only a short time ago you were happy about it,' she accused.

'A short time ago I didn't have an idea that we could be related.' Seeing the puzzlement on her face he continued. 'Do you not see that a relationship between my daughter and your son is too close?'

She relaxed as the import of his words became clear.

'Jamie is not my son,' she assured him.

'He is not your son?' There was disbelief in his tone.

'There is no blood relationship between me and Jamie,' she explained. 'He was the result of a young Papist woman and my first husband when he was in his teens. I didn't know him then of course but I'm told the lassie was a wild one and plagued any man that came near her. After she had the bairn her family whisked her away someplace and I understand that she finished up in a mental home. Jamie was sent to a school of sorts where the teaching was done by nuns. Then he stayed with an uncle for a while but this uncle wanted to marry a strict Calvinist woman and she would have nothing to do with the boy. Seeing he was a Papist of sorts I suppose you can't really blame her. Anyway, he was looking for a job on a boat and both Ruari Beag and Ruari Mor felt it was the right thing to do so they took him aboard *The Two Ruaris*. He used to sleep on the boat, but when the winter came I said it would be too cold for him so we found him a bed in the house here. Jamie was with his father bringing home peats when his father drowned. He dived and swam around for a long time they told me but there was no sign of the body.

'So.' It was more of an ejaculation than a comment.

Kirsty carried on. 'Jamie seemed not to know what to call me but when Wee Ruari started to call me Mam I suppose he liked the idea and asked if I minded if he called me Mam too. Of course I didn't mind so I've been Mam to him for long enough. But his background is well known hereabouts; they take it for granted.'

Hugh Roberton was quiet for a few minutes before he spoke again.

'I guess knowing the full facts makes it easier to ask you something that I've been thinking about.'

'Carry on,' she encouraged.

'I want you to come back to Canada with us.'

'Never! I couldn't possibly leave Westisle,' she declared forcefully.

'Why?' It was just one word quietly spoken yet she felt compelled to give him a full explanation.

'Westisle is mine. I own it. The best part of my life has been spent here and I have grown to love it.'

'You would grow to love Canada too, and there are many things there that would give you an easier and more rewarding life.'

'I am happy with my life here,' she insisted.

'Since it seems you are my half-sister I can remind you that you are not getting any younger,' he chaffed her.

'That is true, I am growing old. I have faced up to that.'

'But I shall want to look after you. And Jamie and Dina will want to look after you also.'

She shook her head negatively and he decided to change the subject.

'Dina and Jamie are going to have a big surprise when they get back and hear the discovery we've made.'

'Do you think they will be pleased?' Kirsty queried.

'I'm sure Dina will be both pleased and delighted. She knows I've been wanting to find a relative in the islands and to learn that it's you will make her ecstatic. It will be a real family celebration.'

'I would sooner you didn't tell her tonight,' she begged. 'Let's sleep on it first. It's been quite a shock to us both, hasn't it?'

'But it will make her so happy it seems mean to keep it from her,' he objected.

'Please. She can know tomorrow.' Kirsty hoped he would not ask for a reason. She couldn't have given him a reason, not then. She simply knew she wanted to hug the knowledge to herself for a few more hours.

'OK,' he yielded. 'Tomorrow. When we're both here together?'

She nodded her agreement.

'You will be coming to Canada of course?' He sounded as though her nod of agreement were a formality.

He had risen and she looked at him startled, wanting to say 'there's no "of course" about it', but she realised that she would want to see Jamie and Dina married.

'If Enac and Euan Ally would be willing to see to things it might be possible for me to come,' she conceded in a murmur.

'I guess Jamie will book passage for you and Wee Ruari at the same time as he books his own. We'll have to get him on to it tomorrow.' His tone was brisk. 'Mind you, he might have already booked his own passage.'

'To Canada!' she said feebly. The words made her wince; they made everything sound so final.

It was midnight when the travellers returned home.

'Did you meet Marney's man?' she asked Jamie.

'Aye, we did that. He's sleeping on the boat tonight,' he told her and in answer to her querulous look added, 'He seems not a bad sort of chap at all.'

'Euan Ally said much the same sort of thing, didn't he?' Dina put in.

'Aye, that's right, he did,' confirmed Jamie. 'Patrick, that's Marney's man, is well used to boats seein' his father had a fishing boat in Ireland where he comes from; they lost the boat in a storm so he came to Scotland to look for a job. He worked on a farm for a while but then he got in with a crooked lot in Glasgow.'

'I guess Marney was fairly upset when she saw him.'

'There were quite a few tears,' Dina said.

'I reckon Patrick shed a few too,' said Jamie. 'But they soon had their arms round each other and they seemed happy enough. Marney and the twins are going to show him the island tomorrow and she wants him to come and see you.'

'He'll be welcome,' Kirsty agreed cordially.

The next morning when Dina came down to a late breakfast she was carrying a parcel which she handed to Kirsty before sitting down.

'Pop gave me some money so I could bring you a present from Canada,' she explained. 'It's from him and from me.'

'For me,' Kirsty exclaimed. 'Am I to look at it now?'

Dina nodded and watched critically as Kirsty unfolded the silky green blouse and held it up for inspection.

'I hope you like it,' said Dina. 'Pop does; he says it will show off your hair.'

Kirsty was conscious of her cheeks growing warm and knew she must be flushing. 'It is very kind of you and your father,' she tried to make her voice sound enthusiastic. 'But it's not really the sort of thing I can wear here.'

Dina's expression clouded. 'You don't like it?'

'I think it is very nice indeed,' Kirsty hastily assured her. 'And I am very grateful to you for giving it to me.' What could one say when one was given a present that, no matter how nice it was, one knew one would never be able to wear? Her mouth was too dry to continue.

'I hope you and Wee Ruari will come to Canada for my wedding. It really is a wonderful country,' said Dina.

'You and Jamie will be waiting until you get back to Canada before you get married?'

'That is what we plan to do,' Dina admitted. 'We've talked it over and Jamie was sure we could persuade you to come.'

173

'You will have plenty of friends coming to your wedding. I doubt you will need my presence.'

'There'll be lots of friends coming to my wedding,' Dina confirmed. 'But none that we will want to be there more than you.' Then, as the door was pushed back and her father came into the room, 'Oh, there you are Pop! Where have you been?'

'I took a walk over to the "Castle" to see Enac,' he replied. 'There was something I needed to talk over with her.'

He looked at Kirsty. 'Are we going to let her into our secret?'

Kirsty nodded. 'You can tell her,' she agreed.

'What secret have you got Pop?' Dina asked eagerly.

'Well, to start things off I have to tell you that Jamie is not Kirsty's son.'

'Oh that's no secret. Jamie told me a while ago.' She seemed disappointed.

'So! You didn't tell me,' her father accused.

'I didn't think it was important,' Dina replied combatively.

'Then the big secret is that Kirsty and I have discovered we are, almost certainly I'd say, half-brother and sister. That's important isn't it?' he smiled triumphantly.

'Pop!' Dina squeaked. Jumping up from her chair she hugged first Kirsty and then her father. 'That's wonderful. How did you manage to discover it?'

'Painstaking research,' he replied, with a wink at Kirsty. 'You know well enough how keen I've been to find a relative in these parts.'

'Jamie doesn't know yet?' Dina asked eagerly.

'Jamie doesn't know, nor does anyone else,' her father confirmed.

'You'll leave it to me to tell Jamie? Promise!'

'I guess we'll leave it to you,' he conceded.

'Jamie will be as thrilled as I am. He'll be even more certain now that Kirsty will make a home in Canada with us.'

'I have a home here,' Kirsty reminded them. 'I would not wish to have another home in Canada.'

Wee Ruari emerged from his bedroom as she was speaking. 'I would wish to,' he piped up but Kirsty, placing a bowl of porridge in front of him, hushed him into quietness.

On her way to the cattle that morning she called in for a 'wee crack' with Enac. Marney was helping her with the loom.

'So you'll be going out to Canada for Jamie's wedding?' Enac greeted her.

'I'd have to ask you to look after the cattle and the hens?'

'Oh, we'd be happy to do that,' Enac offered without hesitation. 'But I'm after thinking you'd need some new clothes for travelling.'

'I still have my Burberry,' Kirsty told her. 'I know it's years old but it's still good.'

Enac gave her a crumpled smile. 'I reckon you'll be saying you've still got your old black beret but that's no good for going to Canada. You'll need to get a new hat, and a new hat won't go with an old Burberry.' There was a challenge in her words.

'Maybe not,' Kirsty accepted. 'But where will I get a hat unless I crochet one for myself?'

Enac pulled open a drawer. 'I've got a couple of catalogues here that I've saved just to have a look at from time to time. Maybe you'll find something in them that'll suit you.'

Kirsty took the catalogues from Enac. 'I'll take a good look at them this evening,' she promised.

As she made her way homeward she let herself dwell on the possibility of getting some new clothes. Mentally she wanted to dismiss the notion of new clothes as resolutely as she had at first dismissed the idea of going to Canada, but when Dina came in that evening and they were chatting after supper was cleared away she produced the catalogues.

'Enac thought I might get one or two things to wear,' she said timidly.

Dina glanced at them carelessly.

'You buy clothes from these?' she asked.

'Only when the tinkers have nothing to suit me when they come with their bales to Clachan.'

Dina looked at her with unconcealed dismay.

'Underclothes I mean,' Kirsty explained hurriedly. 'I knit my own jerseys and I have my good skirt that was made from a length of tweed woven by Enac's mother. It will never wear out.'

'What about a hat?' Dina wanted to know.

'What happens usually is when there's a wedding or something like that and folks feel they need to wear a hat they get together with a few catalogues and each of them orders one or two that they might like. Then they get a chance to pass all of them round and try them on and then they can choose the one that suits them best,' Kirsty explained.

'So!' Dina was non-committal. They sat down together and discussed various items illustrated in the catalogues and eventually decided which Kirsty should send for.

'How long will it take for them to come?' Dina was anxious to know.

'Depends on weather conditions,' Kirsty replied. 'Maybe two weeks, maybe even three!'

'Tell the firm they're urgent,' counselled Dina. 'And I suggest you start crocheting a beret of sorts to wear with your new coat when it comes.'

So, her wardrobe was ordered and she was going to Canada. Kirsty could now convince herself but she wondered if there would be time to arrange everything else that needed to be done.

When the end of the week came and 'the boys' were back from their fishing they all gathered for a 'crack', Enac and her baby, Euan Ally, Marney and her man Patrick. A bottle of whisky was soon produced, along with several of Irn-Bru for the children. Kirsty hadn't met Marney's man until that evening but she was favourably impressed. He struck her as being a nice enough fellow and it was obvious that he was fond his family. When the first stiffness had been shed and they had grown easy with one another he turned to her.

'Call me Patrick,' he told her and went on, 'Me and Marney are wondering if you would mind us cutting a few sods to stack against the windward side of the tent? It would make it kind of cosier for the bairns.'

'And for us too,' Marney reminded him.

'Of course I don't object,' Kirsty assured him. Her eyes widened as she looked at him and Marney; her hand went to her throat as the idea formed swiftly in her mind. Voicelessly she continued watching them until she caught Hugh Roberton's quizzical smile. He seemed to be intrigued

177

by her quirkish behaviour, and she managed to find her voice.

'Enac,' she began. 'Since you are going to look after this place for me would you agree to come and live here in this house? Then you could let Marney and Patrick live in the "Castle", couldn't you?'

Everyone seemed stunned for a few minutes and then Euan Ally turned to Jamie. 'You want to have your say now,' he encouraged.

'Aye indeed. Listen Mam,' Jamie began. 'I want to tell you that Patrick has been fishing with us this past week and Euan Ally's thinking to take him on to work *The Two Ruaris*. He's good at the job and Euan Ally's mighty pleased to have him aboard.'

Startled Kirsty looked from one to the other.

'And are you content?' Her question was directed at Jamie, who nodded emphatically.

'It seems that it's all settled then,' she announced, and with that the three men got up and shook hands with each other. Hugh Roberton jumped up to join in and in a moment they were all shaking hands and kissing, even the children.

'A real celebration,' Hugh Roberton exclaimed. 'And I think that this is a good time to tell you all that Kirsty and I are half-brother and sister!'

There were more congratulations, more hugs and kisses, and at the end of the night everyone went home full of good humour and warmed with whisky and Irn-Bru.

Kirsty was up before anyone the next morning and once she had lit the fire and made porridge, she fed the hens, leaving herself time to go and sit alone on her favourite shelf of rock. There she stored the dawn-fresh scents in her memory. A shower, almost too fine to be perceptible, came with a breath of wind from the sea. She lifted her chin and tossed back her hair.

'Tomorrow,' she promised herself, 'tomorrow I'll get Jamie to take me over to Clachan to see the factor about Marney's man. And I can visit the lairs where Ruari Beag and Ruari Mor are buried and say my final farewells to them.'

Her final farewells! She jolted herself into reality. She would be coming back of course. Wouldn't she? Her conscious mind refused to accept any other possibility, but as she walked back to the house her thoughts were in turmoil.

There was no one about when she arrived so she brewed a pot of tea and sat down to drink a cup. Hugh Roberton was the first to come downstairs.

'No one else up yet?' he queried.

'No, Jamie's recovering from too much excitement or too much whisky. He puts in a hard enough day usually so I leave him alone when he chooses to take things easy.'

'Seeing we're alone then, I want to ask you to seriously consider coming out to live in Canada,' he began. 'I want you to be my housekeeper. I have a nice enough house and there are all sorts of gadgets for making life easier and there'd be help if you wanted it.'

She treated him to a gentle smile though she was shaking her head negatively.

'No,' she said. 'You are still a youngish man Hugh, and it occurs to me that you might wish to marry again. A housekeeper would be in the way then.'

His jaw hardened. 'I forbid you ever to speak to me again on that subject, Kirsty.' His voice was stern and inflexible.

'I adored my wife and I can never consider attaching myself to another woman. I swear she was truly my world, so never speak that way again please.'

She saw his tight-clasped hands and restrained herself from a murmur of sympathy. They were both sitting quietly when Jamie came into the room.

'Jamie, would you consider taking me over to Clachan tomorrow? I would like to see the factor about a croft for Patrick.' She didn't mention that she wanted to visit the lairs.

'Surely,' he replied. 'Anyone else fancy the trip?'

'I'll go and ask Dina,' volunteered Hugh Roberton. 'I guess she'd like to go.'

Next day when they set out across the Sound, the sky was blue and spread with thin white clouds that looked like combed tresses of silvery hair, and the breeze was pushing the sea into white wavelets. The others accompanied Kirsty on the bus trip to the village where the factor had his office, but when they suggested meeting at the hotel for a meal she made the excuse that she needed to visit the cobbler. Having completed her business with the factor, however, she found the cobbler's tiny cluttered shop closed so she set off for the lairs.

It was a dreary place and obviously little attempt was made to keep it tidy. She had taken a bunch of heather from Westisle, but first she knelt to stroke the soft green grass that covered the mound. How much goodness and kindness lay there she meditated. How much love they had left behind. Women were not tolerated at burials in the lairs so she had not been present when the two Ruaris had been laid to rest but the sadness reasserted itself chillingly. Again she prayed, 'Why, Dear God, why?' knowing that countless folk asked themselves the same question time after time, year after lifelong year.

Resolutely she straightened herself, scattered the heather on the grave and wished the two Ruaris farewell.

After walking the mile or two to where the bus left for Clachan she found the others already waiting.

'We've fairly enjoyed ourselves,' said Jamie. 'Did you?'

'The factor is always very pleasant,' she replied primly. 'And he always gives me a cup of tea.'

The clothes she'd ordered from the catalogue arrived the following week. Dina supervised the trying on while Enac and Marney voiced their somewhat unenthusiastic approval. That night, when Hugh Roberton announced that he and Dina would be leaving the island en route for Canada at the end of the week, Kirsty experienced a sense of breathlessness. Jamie had already told her that he had booked their passages for the week following the Robertons' departure. Her mind seemed to be in a confusion of dread and anticipation. She resolved to try to calm herself by collecting a few mementos she would like to take with her so she set out across the moors to gather one or two of the blooming wild flowers, intending to press them between the pages of an album along with a grouse feather and a fringe of hair from their Highland bull. Wee Ruari, with the help of the twins, proposed to gather shells and seaweed.

All too soon the day of departure came. Enac was prepared to move into the house and had been told to use the contents of the chest which the mother of the two Ruaris had set aside. The other chest which Ruari Mor had said was hers was packed and locked and ready for transport to Canada if she should send word that she required it.

Euan Ally and Patrick were taking Jamie, Kirsty and Wee Ruari on *The Two Ruaris* to the port, where they would spend the night with the postmistress before catching the early train to Glasgow. There, they would embark on the liner that would take them to Canada.

There was only a light wind and Kirsty stood outside the wheelhouse of *The Two Ruaris* enclosed by a sense of timelessness. She watched each cliff loom up from a thin attendant mist, supplicatingly it seemed to her, before allowing itself to merge once more into the familiar outline of the island.

The scene touched her heart, and Wee Ruari standing beside her reached for her hand.

'You're not crying are you?' he demanded.

'No, no,' she denied. 'Are you?'

He shook his head.

'They'll still be there when we come back won't they?' he asked wistfully.

She looked at him and smiled.

'They'll still be there,' she assured him.

LILLIAN BECKWITH

THE BAY OF STRANGERS

In these eight short stories Lillian Beckwith packs in a rich cast of characters and seductive Highland settings. In the title story Catriona McRae embarks on married life and learns a closely guarded secret from her mother-in-law. 'The Banjimolly' features a witch – and two bottles of whisky. 'Because of an Elephant' concerns an eccentric laird's wife. A boy and his adored collie dog, Meg, are the subjects of 'The Last Shot'. Each story is beautifully and affectionately told.

BEAUTIFUL JUST!

On the Hebridean island of Bruach, life among the crofters is as happy and full of humour as ever. Beckwith tells enchanting tales about the islanders' wit, their canny resourcefulness and their gossipy interest in outsiders. There is Flora and the fancy-dress dance, beachcombing, winkle-gathering, Highland cattle and a stag – among many other characters and animals. Based on Beckwith's own experiences.

'Hilarious' – *The Sunday Times*

'Absorbing...its humour is happy, easy and natural'
– *The Mirror*

LILLIAN BECKWITH

BRUACH BLEND

Meet some familiar – and some less familiar – inhabitants
of Bruach. Back with more comical escapades are Erchy and
Morag, the philandering Hector and Hamish, with his
unusual talent for nursing lambs. We meet also Bonny the
cow, Crumley the bull, and Harry the hedgehog which
make up 'Miss Peckwitt's colourful and uncontrollable
collection of animals and other livestock'.

'A book which leaves you with a warm, happy glow. Her
Highland crofters emerge from the pages as true friends'
– *The Mirror*

'How can anyone read this book without being convulsed
with laughter and admiration?' – *Eastern Daily Press*

THE HILLS IS LONELY

When Lillian Beckwith advertised for a secluded place
in the country, she received a letter with the following
unusual description of an isolated Hebridean croft: 'Surely
it's that quiet even the sheeps themselves on the hills is
lonely and as to the sea it's that near as I use it myself
everyday for the refusals...'

Her curiosity aroused, Beckwith took up the invitation.
This is the comic and enchanting story of the strange rest-
cure that followed and her efforts to adapt to a completely
different way of life.

'A bouquet for Miss Beckwith' – Eric Linklater

LILLIAN BECKWITH

THE LOUD HALO

In *The Loud Halo* Lillian Beckwith serves up another delightful slice of Hebridean life and a collection of local characters. Meet Johnny Comic, Morag, Kirsty, Behag, Hector, Erchy and the postie – among others. Subjects for amusement include tourists, an election, blizzards and a tinker's wedding. Each episode is told with wit and affection.

'A sparkling book which could well become a Scottish humorous classic' – *Weekly Scotsman*

THE SEA FOR BREAKFAST

Lillian Beckwith's settling in on the island of Bruach and having a croft of her own, is the basis of these comic adventures. Adapting to a totally different way of life provides many excuses for humour and the eccentric cast of characters guarantees there is never a dull moment on Bruach. In one story beachcombing yields a strange find. In another a Christmas party results in a riotous night's celebrations.

'The most amusing book to come my way'
– *The Sunday Times*

'It would be very difficult not to enjoy *The Sea for Breakfast*...for the charm and simplicity of its writing, not to mention the wonderful, warm people who inhabit its covers' – *The Scotsman*

PAYMENT

Please tick currency you wish to use:

☐ £ (Sterling)　　☐ $ (US)　　☐ $ (CAN)　　☐ € (Euros)

Allow for shipping costs charged per order plus an amount per book as set out in the tables below:

CURRENCY/DESTINATION

	£(Sterling)	$(US)	$(CAN)	€(Euros)
Cost per order				
UK	1.50	2.25	3.50	2.50
Europe	3.00	4.50	6.75	5.00
North America	3.00	3.50	5.25	5.00
Rest of World	3.00	4.50	6.75	5.00
Additional cost per book				
UK	0.50	0.75	1.15	0.85
Europe	1.00	1.50	2.25	1.70
North America	1.00	1.00	1.50	1.70
Rest of World	1.50	2.25	3.50	3.00

PLEASE SEND CHEQUE OR INTERNATIONAL MONEY ORDER
payable to: HOUSE OF STRATUS LTD or card payment as indicated

STERLING EXAMPLE

Cost of book(s):..................... Example: 3 x books at £6.99 each: £20.97
Cost of order:...................... Example: £1.50 (Delivery to UK address)
Additional cost per book:.............. Example: 3 x £0.50: £1.50
Order total including shipping:.......... Example: £23.97

VISA, MASTERCARD, SWITCH, AMEX:

☐ ☐ ☐ ☐ ☐ ☐ ☐ ☐ ☐ ☐ ☐ ☐ ☐ ☐ ☐ ☐ ☐ ☐ ☐ ☐

Issue number (Switch only):

☐ ☐ ☐

Start Date:　　　　　　**Expiry Date:**

☐ ☐ / ☐ ☐　　　　　☐ ☐ / ☐ ☐

Signature: _____

NAME: _____

ADDRESS: _____

COUNTRY: _____

ZIP/POSTCODE: _____

Please allow 28 days for delivery. Despatch normally within 48 hours.

Prices subject to change without notice.
Please tick box if you do not wish to receive any additional information. ☐

House of Stratus publishes many other titles in this genre; please check our website (**www.houseofstratus.com**) for more details.